SIXTH STREET LOVE AFFAIR

A THREE RIVERS RANCH ROMANCE BOOK 5

LIZ ISAACSON

AEJ
CREATIVE WORKS

Copyright © 2020 by Elana Johnson, writing as Liz Isaacson

All rights reserved.

No part of this book may be reproduced in any form or by any electronic or mechanical means, including information storage and retrieval systems, without written permission from the author, except for the use of brief quotations in a book review.

ISBN-13: 978-1-953506-14-6

SCRIPTURE

"Wait on the Lord: be of good courage, and He shall strengthen thine heart: wait, I say, on the Lord."

Psalms 27:14

CHAPTER ONE

The confines around Juliette Thompson's heart had never been so weary. Of course, she hadn't travelled to Montana for a wedding alone, where the man she had a crush on had brought another woman, in well, ever.

It's your own fault, she told herself as she watched Garth and his summer sweetheart—Gwen, or Jenn, or was it Jenna?—stand and inch their way down the aisle toward the airplane's exit.

They hadn't booked the same flight north, because Juliette had flown in as late as possible for her nephew's wedding. But as her luck would have it, she and Garth-plus-one were on the same plane back to Texas. And she'd had an aisle seat only a few rows behind them, a birds-eye view for everything they did. If Garth had seen her—and recognized her with her new blonde locks—he hadn't acknowledged her.

Not that she blamed him for that, either. She sighed as she reached into the overhead compartment for her carryon, determined to duck into the first available Cinnabon shop and drown her self-loathing in frosting and gooey bread. That should give Garth and GwenJenn a chance to get out of the airport, lessening the probability that Juliette would have to face him.

She'd have to soon enough, anyway. He seemed to call the veterinary clinic where she worked a couple times a month, and since she'd worked with the animals at Three Rivers for so long, Doctor Bent always asked Juliette to go.

That was how her infatuation had begun with the tall, mysterious Garth Ahlstrom. She'd had her eye on him during those few visits each month, but the ranch and the construction on Courage Reins kept his attention elsewhere.

How was she to know he'd been her previous husband's friend? She'd never met any of Brad's friends— he'd made sure of that. But by the time Juliette had made the connection, she'd already started something with Garth she didn't want to end.

But end it she had. Decisively. Even if Garth continued to call and come over after church for her Texas barbeque. After a few weeks, he'd stopped, widening the hole in her heart that had been there since her marriage ended nearly a decade earlier.

She ordered a caramel pecanbon, already in a diabetic coma just from the smell inside the shop. Once she had her tasty treat, she found a table in the corner where she could watch the airport travelers inconspicuously.

She wasn't sure why she cared—Garth and Girlfriend had gotten off the plane several passengers ahead of her, but she took her time devouring the roll, mostly to waste minutes before she had to drive home to her empty house. Well, she did have two dogs and a cat who would be excited to see her.

Juliette had loved animals since age three, when her dad—once the foreman at Horseshoe Home Ranch in Montana, where her nephew Tom now worked—had brought home their first family dog. A golden retriever, Minnie had charmed everyone, most of all Juliette.

She'd earned her veterinarian technician degree the year she'd married Brad, and she'd been happy to have the certification when she left Montana for good. She usually never stayed in one place for more than a couple of years, though she'd been in Three Rivers for three now.

She'd chosen the small Texas town because Tom lived here, making it the last place Brad would think she'd gone. Most people on the run avoided places where their family lived.

Then Garth Ahlstrom had entered the picture. As far as Juliette knew, he didn't know about their mutual connection through Brad. And she'd like to keep it that way.

"You're too old for him anyway," she muttered as she got up and put her cardboard tray in the trashcan. Yet another lie she told herself to keep the walls around her heart from collapsing. After all, the man was thirty-two, only three years her junior.

She drove the distance from Amarillo to Three Rivers, the radio on loud so her thoughts couldn't settle onto one topic for too long. She pulled into town, a soft sigh escaping her throat. Three Rivers had captivated her from the first moment she'd visited several years ago.

Then, she'd flown under a false identity, with fake papers she'd spent hundreds of dollars to get. Brad didn't know where she'd gone then, and he didn't know where she lived now. It was the only way she'd been able to escape the marriage, escape him.

She reminded herself of this—of why Garth couldn't know she'd once been Juli Thornton, devoted wife to the largest rodeo winner on the PRCA circuit. Devoted wife who suffered under his brutal fists whenever he wasn't on the road.

Juliette shook her head to dislodge the memories that had crept up on her. She passed the elementary school, the familiar pang to have a family still as sharp as ever beneath her breastbone. Brad hadn't wanted children, and he'd beaten her so severely once, Juliette wasn't even sure she could have a baby.

With night closing in fast, Juliette stopped admiring the tall trees and green spaces in Three Rivers, the shops she loved to visit on the weekends, her favorite New York-style deli, and focused on getting home.

She turned on Sixth Street, the motion so automatic she didn't have to think. She slammed on the brakes a moment later, not having seen the navy vehicle just around the corner, idling on the curb.

Juliette pulled the wheel to the left to avoid hitting the truck. The truck that was all too familiar....

Her sedan came to a screeching stop just as Garth got out of his truck. He wore the smile that made Juliette's insides dance, but she refused to let herself return it. He motioned for her to roll down the window, but she set her mouth in a straight line and shook her head.

She tapped her wrist like she had an ultra-important appointment to get to—on a Sunday evening—and put her car in drive. Not that it mattered. She lived only three doors down and by the time she'd pulled into her carport, Garth stood in the driveway.

"Evenin', ma'am." He tipped his hat to her, another cowboy behavior she happened to adore.

"What are you doing here?"

He gestured down the road. "Jenny's mother lives on the corner. She wanted me to drop her there."

Juliette didn't know how to answer. She certainly didn't know everyone in Three Rivers, but she'd never met the blonde woman Garth had touted to Montana.

She tossed her own bottle-blonde hair over her shoulder, biting back an invitation for him to come in for coffee. She'd already had sixteen ounces at the Cinnabon—as her bladder was suddenly reminding her.

"So you and Jenny?" She hated the jealous undertones in her question.

He shrugged. "Maybe." He glanced over his shoulder

like the woman would be standing there. "But probably not."

Juliette couldn't ignore the swelling of happiness in her chest, the press of it almost eliciting a smile from her. She caught it just in time. "Well, I have to go in."

He took a few quick strides forward. "Why?"

She looked back at him, trying to formulate an answer. "Because Teddy and Grant need me." The dogs. She could always use them as an excuse. "I only paid my sitter to come this morning."

"I'm sorry about Betsy Ross." He ducked his head and ran his fingertips along the brim of his cowboy hat, a sign of his emotion.

Sudden sadness clogged her throat. "She was in a lot of pain." Juliette missed the exuberant great Dane who'd died of cancer over the summer. She'd wished Garth had been in her life, that she hadn't ended things with him, that she knew how to apologize and fix things between them.

"Did you fly home tonight?" he asked, cocking his head at her. She had a love-hate relationship with the way he looked at her. She loved the heat he always carried in his eyes, the slow smolder she was sure would incinerate if she'd allow him to touch her. She hated the way he seemed to be able to penetrate her carefully crafted defenses with such a simple gaze.

"Yes," she said. "You?"

"We were on the same flight, Juliette." He took another step forward. "I saw you."

"Really?" She backed up a pace when she realized how near he'd come. All the way into the carport, to the backdoor on the sedan. "I didn't see—"

"Yes, you did." He stuffed his hands in his pockets and stayed put. Thankfully. "Your hair looks nice. Different. But nice."

"Thank you." She didn't know what else to say, so she scrambled up the few steps that led to the house. If she could just get inside, she wouldn't have to see him, smell him, succumb to him.

"Well, good night." She twisted the key in the lock and pushed open the door. She stepped inside and firmly shut it behind her, leaving Garth in her carport. Resisting the urge to tiptoe to her living room and watch through the blinds until he left, she instead moved through the kitchen and dining room and turned into the laundry room. Teddy and Grant started wagging their tails, and Juliette let the dogs out of their kennels. The dogs who were always happy to see her, never expected her to tell them things she'd rather not.

Garth stood in Juliette's carport, wondering how much strength it would take to bust down a locked door. That would probably be the easy part of getting Juliette to talk to him. Really talk to him. Tell him why things between them seemed to be going just fine until that fateful day in April.

Three months had passed since then. Three painful months of sitting by himself at church, of attending the community picnics with a large group instead of enjoying a private feast in Juliette's backyard.

The worst part was Garth didn't even know what he'd done wrong. What he'd said to drive her away. He couldn't remember what they'd spoken about, or where they'd gone, or anything. One day she was hot, the next day cold. And now, blonde.

He turned away from her door the same way he turned off his thoughts. He'd have to repent for lying to her about why he was parked at the end of her street. He seemed to have a love affair with Sixth Street, and he didn't want her to know how often he'd parked there, waiting for her to leave simply so he could catch a glimpse of her.

He didn't need to add *stalker* to his rap sheet, that was for certain. His cowboy boots made angry clunking sounds as he crossed the pavement and jumped into his still idling truck. He'd driven fast from Amarillo to Three Rivers, dropped Jenny at her house on the other side of town, and high-tailed it here so he could see Juliette when she got home. She'd taken a long time, and he'd had to turn on his truck so he didn't die from the heat inside the cab.

He aimed the truck toward the ranch, suddenly desperate to get back to his cabin. Going to Montana, even for a visit, had unsettled him. Reminded him of everything he'd worked these last two years to forget. Everyone he needed to leave in the past.

Physically leaving his wife behind had been hard when he'd done it two years ago. Making room for someone else in his life mentally, emotionally, and spiritually was proving to be ten times more difficult.

He'd started the process with Juliette, and he'd thought maybe he really was ready to open his heart again. He hadn't compared Juliette to Kim, hadn't thought of Kim when he was with Juliette, hadn't told Juliette about Kim.

"So I still have some guards in place," he muttered to himself. "Big deal." But intellectually, he knew his barriers were a big deal. Knew his style of communication—stalking and short conversations—created an obstacle he'd have to fix at some point.

Garth parked next to his cabin and went inside. He'd left it clean, and since he'd been gone for a few days, the items on his ranch to-do list would be a mile long. His personal to-do list only contained one thing: sleep.

But he couldn't do that very well, especially since the day didn't seem to fade into full darkness until close to midnight. He found himself on the back porch, his dog, Leo, at his feet, staring at the range.

A pang of longing for snow hit him unexpectedly. He'd hated the snow in Montana, but Kim had loved it. When she'd been diagnosed, her one wish had been to live to see another winter. She'd made it through Christmas and the New Year, something Garth thanked the Lord for every day of his life. He hadn't wanted to associate his wife's death with the holidays and relive it every year. Her death in January had definitely made his life easier.

He scratched Leo's ears as he chuckled to himself. Like burying Kim during a Montana January had been easy.

Garth brought Leo into his cabin when he finally felt tired enough to fall asleep. The hound started snoring before Garth did, but he eventually drifted into unconsciousness, taking Juliette's slim figure, bright blue eyes, and quick wit with him.

He woke to the sound of pounding fists on his front door and Leo whining in the hallway. Garth stumbled through his dark cabin, sure he'd only slept for a few minutes. His brain felt foggy and his muscles limp as he wrenched open the door.

Ethan, his best cowhand, stood there, worry etched all over his face. "Coyotes, boss. Two bulls are down. Haven't been able to account for all the cattle yet."

The haze in Garth's mind evaporated. "Call the vet. I'll be out in two minutes." He returned to his bedroom for a pair of jeans and a fresh pair of socks. It only took him sixty seconds to be ready, and he hurried down his steps and around the admin trailer, where he found Ethan on the phone.

"Doc's callin' Juliette now," he said after he hung up.

Even as Ethan led Garth to the bullpen in the nearby pasture to assess the wounds on the two bulls, he couldn't help smiling. Juliette couldn't avoid him if it was her job to come out to Three Rivers Ranch.

CHAPTER TWO

*A*fter the long forty-minute drive out to the ranch, Juliette eased her car to a stop next to Garth's pickup, her stomach an angry nest of vipers. She'd tried to make an excuse for why she couldn't go out to Three Rivers Ranch in the dead of night, but Doctor Bent hadn't heard a word she'd said.

In the bullpens, she found herself face-to-face with Garth, with only Ethan as a witness to anything they said or did. Luckily, Garth knew how to keep private things private.

"What happened?" She knelt next to him and scanned the animal on the ground. The bull had to weigh at least two thousand pounds and had fresh blood on both back legs. "Did you sedate him?"

"Both of 'em." Garth nodded toward a slightly smaller bull that had chest wounds as well as leg injuries. "Coyotes. A pack of 'em, from what we can tell." He stood and paced away, running his hands under his cowboy hat and through his hair. He said something to Ethan, who nodded and left the bullpen.

Juliette stared at him, wishing she could rake her hands through his hair too. She'd loved his salt-and-pepper hair from the day she'd seen it, which was after several public picnics as the man never removed his hat during working hours. He'd complained about his hair making him look too old and that he was considering coloring it, and she'd told him she liked how distinguished it made him.

He'd never dyed it, something that tickled Juliette though she'd never admit such things out loud.

When his penetrating gaze met hers, she yanked her attention back to the bull. *Caught staring*, she thought. *How embarrassing.* She opened her med kit and reached for a large piece of gauze to determine how bad the bleeding was. Everything looked black against the night, against the bull's dark hair, and she couldn't tell the extent of the damage.

"What do you think, Doc?" Garth joined her, pressing in too close. Probably because she'd opened the door for him with that stupid stare-fest.

"I'm not a doctor," she reminded him. She pressed the gauze against the bull's leg, immediately feeling the warmth of the blood as it seeped into the pad. "But this animal definitely needs one." She pulled a bottle of blood stop powder from her kit. "This is bad, Garth. I'll try to stop the bleeding, but if I can't...." She poured a healthy amount of the powder on the wound, trying to calculate how much was enough as this medicine was usually used on dogs and cats.

She pulled out a hefty cloth and leaned her weight on the bull's leg. After a moment, she pulled it back to check the blood level.

"That's not good," Garth said as he stared at the bloody towel.

"No, it's not." Juliette reapplied pressure and nodded toward the other bull. "Take my powder and pour it on his legs. Get as many towels as you can and let's see if we can't get the bleeding contained."

Garth started to move away, but she called him back. "And Garth? Call David and tell him we need him out here. I can't save these bulls myself."

He gave her a terse nod and strode out of the pen. Juliette leaned on the bull and counted to thirty. Then she heaved her bag over to the other bull and assessed his chest wounds, which were minor injuries she could treat on-site.

She had just finished dressing the chest wounds when Garth arrived with an armful of towels and an army of cowhands.

"Tell 'em what to do, Juliette." He spoke in a calm, authoritative voice, one she'd like to hear say her name on a daily basis. She resisted the impulse to tell him she was sorry, that she'd been lying when she'd told him she wasn't interested in him, took a deep breath, and directed two cowhands to the bull she'd left.

She doused the smaller animal with the clotting powder and assigned several more men to put pressure on the wounds.

Garth's phone rang and he stepped away from her to take the call. She couldn't hear what he said, and the moment he hung up four men on horses thundered into the bullpen.

"Found the herd backed up against the north fences, boss." Ethan swung down off his horse, which another cowboy led to the watering trough. "Several head down." He cast a glance toward Juliette. "No way to save 'em."

Juliette's chest tightened, but she pressed on in her task. She knew what losing cattle meant to a cattle rancher. Even if Garth wasn't the owner of Three Rivers, he'd take the loss personally.

He joined her, his strong shoulders drooping for only the second time she'd ever seen. The first time had been when she'd told him she wasn't interested in seeing him anymore.

"What did—?" she started to ask before her phone began vibrating in her back pocket.

"You want me to get that?" Despite everything, he slid her a sly smile she wished didn't make her want to say yes.

To hide her inner turmoil, she rolled her eyes and snapped her bloody gloves off. She removed her phone in an exaggerated gesture. "It's David." She swiped open the call. "Hello, David."

"Tell me what's going on."

She sighed at his all-business tone, though at two a.m. she didn't want to mince words either. "I think we have the bleeding under control now." She scanned the pen, the bloody towels, the downed bulls. "But there's one bull who needs stitches. The other one I think I can dress and wrap and it'll be okay."

"How serious is it? Can you do it or do I need to come out there?"

The bottom fell out of Juliette's stomach. She hadn't done stitches on an animal this large since, well, since never.

She felt the weight of Garth's eyes on her and found herself saying, "I can do it."

David sighed. "Thank you, Juliette. I'd come right away, but with Erika due any minute now…."

Juliette pressed her eyes closed and took a deliberate breath. "I know, David. I can handle it."

"Take tomorrow off or come in late. Whatever you need."

Juliette gave him a laugh she cut short before her exhaustion and frustration could be heard. "Sure, okay, David. Sounds great. See you later." She hung up and the strength and confidence with which she'd spoken drained from her body.

"So?" Garth asked.

"I need to stitch this one." She exhaled and pointed to the larger bull. "But I'll dress this one first." She pulled on another pair of rubber gloves and got to work, always aware of where Garth was, who he spoke to, if he looked her way.

An hour later, she tied off the last stitch and leaned back on her heels to stretch her back. She felt covered in blood and hair and dirt. Heaviness weighed on her mind and muscles.

"Thank you, Juliette." Garth picked up an armful of towels and threw them in a barrel a cowboy had brought into the pen. "What can I help you with?"

She surveyed the huge mess she'd made with her medical supplies, but she felt like someone had dumped sand in her eyes "I got it." She gathered her tape and gauze as he stooped for her sewing kit.

"I can help."

She realized in that moment that everyone else had vanished into the night, leaving her and Garth alone under the starry sky. Her mind immediately flew to kissing him under this blanket of night, what his hands might feel like cradling her face.

She deliberately moved away to collect a stray gauze wrapper, trying to shove the thoughts out of her traitorous mind. Several minutes later her bag was packed and she was ready to go. She stumbled under the weight of her bag and dropped it to the dirt.

"Hey." Garth stepped into her personal space and steadied her with a hand on her elbow. "Maybe you should stay here."

Juliette's mind clouded with exhaustion. "Where would I sleep?"

"The homestead is empty. Chelsea keeps it air-conditioned and there's hot water. Plenty of beds. You can get on home in the morning."

She glanced over her shoulder, where the buildings in the distance called to her, beckoned to her to stay the night. And it wasn't even a whole night. More like a few hours until the sun made an appearance.

"I don't think you should drive home tonight," Garth said. "I'd feel better if you stayed in the homestead."

Juliette turned to him and tilted her head back to look up at him. His handsomeness struck her full in the heart, and she stepped away, breathless. She swayed on her feet and he swept his arm around her waist.

"That's it. You're staying at the homestead. Come on."

She couldn't tell him that her brush with unconsciousness came from the cut lines of his jaw and his striking gray eyes combined with the longest day of her life, so she let him lead her down the road and back to the ranch.

THE NORMAL NOISES OF CLUCKING CHICKENS and a buzz of activity on the ranch had been muted. Garth appreciated the ranch in the middle of the night, the peacefulness of it.

He led Juliette under the deck to a set of doors that opened without a key. "Chelsea leaves this entrance open." He flashed her a smile. "Sometimes I come here in the middle of the day, just to get away for a few minutes."

Juliette seemed as mute as the ranch, and he gestured her inside the house, wondering if his own brain had stopped operating—because he followed her when he should've just pointed to the bedroom and the nearby bathroom.

"You can stay down here," he said, slipping into rambling mode. "There's two bedrooms and a bathroom." He pulled open the fridge. "There's water in here. I send my boys over here all the time to cool off." He cleared his throat. "Or you can stay upstairs. Loads of beds up there. A couple of bathrooms." Garth forced himself to stop talking.

Juliette looked at him with appreciation in her eyes. He thought he saw something else, something deeper, but she blinked and turned away before he could be sure.

"Thank you," she said. "I'll just stay down here." She hugged herself as if cold, and Garth indicated the thermostat.

"You can adjust the temperature here."

"Great." She rocked back and forth on her heels, and Garth realized she was waiting for him to leave.

"Okay, well, I'll go." But he didn't want to leave, couldn't seem to force his feet to move. Three seconds passed, then five, then ten, and he still hadn't so much as twitched a muscle.

"Garth—"

Her voice unlocked him, and he flew into action. "See you tomorrow, Juli. Thanks for—"

"My name is *not* Juli," she growled, causing him to pause at the door and turn back to her.

"I'm sorry."

"Don't *ever* call me that again."

Garth recoiled from the acid in her tone, the fury on her face. He tipped his hat and ducked out the doorway before he said something else that drove her further from him. On the walk back to his cabin, he puzzled through her reaction to the nickname. It had clearly ignited something in her—not something good, either.

A past issue? he wondered, though he wished he could just let her go. He paused and turned back to the homestead, but the light in the basement couldn't be seen. Juliette definitely had a past issue, Garth just didn't know what it was.

He slept until ten a.m. and the fact that no one woke him meant there weren't any more problems on the ranch. At least not problems the foreman needed to deal with. He showered and headed over to the administration trailer, checking for Juliette's car. It still sat next to his truck, and his spirits lifted that he'd get to see her again.

"There you are," she said from behind him, and he stalled his progress toward the door.

"Here I am." He tossed a grin in her direction, not expecting her to return it but still, a snag of disappointment sang through him when she remained straight-faced.

"Ethan's looking for you." She hooked her thumb toward the bullpen. "He's not sure if he should keep the bulls sedated."

"Well, you're the expert on that," Garth said. "How do they look?"

"They should be separated until they heal." Juliette stepped with him toward the pen. "And the big one—"

"Tony."

"Sure, Tony. He'll need painkillers. David brought them out an hour ago, but he wants to show someone how to administer them."

"Why don't you stay and administer them?" The words left Garth's throat before he could censor them.

Juliette froze, her mouth working but no sound coming out.

"I'm certainly not going to give a bull a shot," Garth continued.

"I don't work here," she called after him.

"Sure you do." He cast her look over her shoulder. "I pay the vet bill." And he'd love to hire her if she had the right qualifications. Squire had another year before he finished his degree, and Garth couldn't wait to have a full-time vet on staff at Three Rivers.

"Garth." David Bent, the veterinarian the ranch lacked, stepped up to Garth and shook his hand.

"Thanks for lending us Juliette last night," Garth said. "She's a real trooper."

"She's the best," David agreed. "And I'm afraid you're going to have her for a bit longer."

"I am?" Garth asked, surprise lifting his eyebrows.

"He is?" Juliette's screech didn't exactly settle Garth's stomach.

David hooked his thumb over his shoulder. "That bull has the beginning stages of pinkeye. Juliette will need to ride out and check the herd."

Garth's stomach swooped, first down to his boots at the mention of pinkeye—not fatal, but the treatment required all cowhands on deck—then up to the back of his throat as he thought about riding with Juliette—alone—out to the north forty to check the herd.

CHAPTER THREE

*J*uliette had barely been able to stomp away from Garth and David, but she'd made it into the barn—where blessedly, no one was shoveling out stalls or filling troughs—so she could fume privately. She also only ever wept when alone. She swiped angrily at a tear as it tried to skate down her face.

Most of the horses lazed about because of the heat. They didn't seem to care about the distraught woman in the corner. Clearing the emotion from her throat, Juliette turned her face to the rafters. *Lord*, she prayed. *Help me find the strength to do my job. Help me keep my secret.*

Her thoughts strayed to Garth, but she quickly reeled them in. She would not pray about him. She'd already sworn off relationships. Especially relationships with cowboys.

Her resolve firmly in place, she started to return to the bullpen. Surely David could stay. The ranch had great cell service, and she'd been here most of the night, and his veterinary clinic really couldn't run without her.

"Juliette." Garth's voice came from the shadows to her right, and echoed through the barn with tonalities of caring, compassion, concern. Everything she wished he wouldn't infuse into his voice so easily.

She spun toward him, her fury flying forward with full force. "What do you want from me?"

He shook his head, burying his features beneath his cowboy hat as he ducked his chin to his chest. "Nothing, Juliette. Why don't you get on home and I'll see you… when I see you."

She didn't wait for him to offer again. She marched out of the barn and straight to her car, leaving Garth to explain the situation to *her* boss. She cared about her job, but she couldn't go back. Alone on the dirt road that led from the ranch to the highway, she let her tears tickle her cheeks.

She wasn't even sure why she was crying. Nerves, maybe, at being so close to Garth for so long. Exhaustion, though she'd slept relatively well at the homestead. No matter why, the physicality of the tears alerted her to her possibly insane behavior.

Juliette slammed on her brakes, causing her sedan to fishtail in the loose dirt. She came to rest, her tears drying up instantly. "You're doing it again." She glanced at herself in the rearview mirror. "This is your life. Yours. If you want to go home, go home. If you want to go treat the pinkeye, go treat the pinkeye."

She stared at herself, her brain battling with her heart. It would be unwise to get involved with someone who knew Brad.

Heart: Garth doesn't live in Montana anymore. He's never mentioned Brad.

Brain: Where do you think this relationship can go, Juliette?

Heart: I think I deserve to be happy, Juli.

She took a deep breath, the inward war still raging. She pulled her phone from the console where she'd tossed it and dialed David.

"David," she said by way of greeting. "I don't know if Garth told you, but I'm heading home for a shower and to pack some clothes. I'll stop by the clinic and get the supplies we need for the pinkeye, and I'll be back out to the ranch in a couple of hours."

She rushed through the delivery, hoping none of the turmoil bubbling inside had made it into the syllables she'd said.

"Haven't seen Garth," David said, sounding distracted. "The bulls started to wake, so I sent someone to find him."

Relief cascaded through Juliette like water falling from a cliff. "Can you let him know I'll be back in a little while?" She pressed her eyes closed, took a deep breath, and reminded herself that *she* controlled her life.

"Sure, Juliette. I might not be here when you get back. I don't know how we'll manage at the clinic without you, but we'll make it work. I'm assuming you'll be gone for several days?"

She knew the ranch spanned half a million acres, but

she didn't know how far they'd need to go to find the infected herd. "Ask Garth," she said.

"Will do."

She hung up, a measure of calmness behind her actions as she put the car in drive and continued back to town. Rebuilding the walls around her heart required constant attention, and she spent the forty-minute drive to town doing the best she could to reconstruct the barriers she'd put in place when she'd left Brad.

That had been the hardest thing she'd ever done. She'd escaped in the dead of winter, in the darkest, deepest part of the night. She'd seen Brad at the airport the next day and successfully avoided him. She'd moved eight times in the past ten years.

She could handle riding out on the range with Garth Ahlstrom, even if his good looks and calm personality made her stomach quake.

THE SILENCE AT HER HOUSE SENT PEACE through her soul. She'd always liked the quietness of small towns. Over the few years of her tumultuous marriage, the silent times were the times she was alone, the times she didn't have to worry about Brad coming home inebriated, the times she could find herself lurking in the corners of her mind and remind herself that she had worth.

She paused and leaned against the closed door that led

to the carport, relishing this silence. This silence she'd bought with her fake IDs and careful, inconspicuous living.

Teddy barked, a single yip that inquired when she was going to come let him out. She crossed through the kitchen and entered the laundry room. She freed the dogs from their kennel, instantly engulfed in lapping tongues and whapping tails. She laughed with her dogs and then shoved their faces back.

"Go on, guys." She stepped to the back door to let them out and they tore into the yard with the enthusiasm only two big dogs could achieve.

She wished she could run as freely as they did, could throw all her secrets to the skies and not care where they landed and who found them.

She turned away from Grant and Teddy and headed into her bedroom to pack. Times this trying made Juliette yearn to be able to call her mother, or her sister. An aunt. A friend would suffice.

But Juliette had eliminated everyone who mattered to her. She couldn't risk someone slipping and saying something to Brad. She wouldn't jeopardize them either. So she hadn't spoken to her mother in nearly a decade, and the two sisters she'd left behind in Montana lived lives she knew nothing about. She had acquaintances at work and church, not friends. She kept everyone on a leash, never allowing them to get too close.

Except for Garth. She'd let him in, and it had felt so good. So good to have someone to laugh with. So good to have someone speak to her with tenderness, ask her questions because he was interested in getting to know her, call just to hear her voice.

Garth had done everything right, and she knew her sudden termination of their budding romance had hurt and puzzled him. She tossed a pair of jeans into a backpack and moved to her dresser for socks. She didn't know how to get back what she'd once had with Garth—at least not without telling him things she couldn't.

She placed a bottle of painkillers—for humans, not animals—in the front pocket of her backpack, sure she'd need them later. After all, dealing with Garth usually gave her a headache.

As she headed out the door, she wondered if maybe, just maybe, Garth could be trusted with the blackest part of her life.

AFTER JULIETTE LEFT, A CONSTANT CLOUD seemed to follow Garth wherever he went. He stormed to the homestead, only to find several cowboys there, taking a much-needed break.

He'd left them and headed back into the barn, hoping to find comfort and solace with the horses. But Pete was there, instructing a new assistant in how to work with therapy equines.

"Afternoon, Garth." Pete nodded at him, and Garth stalled his strides toward the exit.

"Pete," he said as if just now realizing Pete was there. Pete, who had worked the ranch as long as Garth had been here. Pete, who had made hard decisions of his own. Pete, who had fallen for Chelsea, married her, and now had a family.

"Pete," he said again, louder this time.

"What's up, Boss?"

Garth glanced at the other man and back to Pete, the message clear. "I have to go out on the range today. Doc said the bulls have pinkeye, and we have to go check the herd."

Pete studied him in that calculated, Army manner he possessed. "And?"

"The horses aren't at risk of getting infected."

"Okay." Pete cocked his head, and Garth wished he could communicate telepathically. A horse snuffled behind them, and Pete gestured to it. "Why don't you go check on him, Paul?"

The other man moved away, and Pete stepped closer. "What's really wrong, Garth?"

Garth needed advice, and at this point, he'd take it from anyone. "How did you get Chelsea to talk to you?"

The seriousness in Pete's face evaporated and a chuckle escaped his mouth. "This is a woman problem? I shoulda known."

Embarrassment crept through Garth, but he derailed it. "There's someone, yes," he said. "We were gettin' along just fine, great even, and then…." Garth trailed off, unsure of what to say.

"Then what?"

"Then she told me to stop coming around. Stopped talking to me completely." Garth thought of the few times he'd sat on the end of her street, hoping for a glimpse of her, waiting to hear her voice as she called to her dogs in her backyard.

"Hmm." Pete glanced around the barn like the mysteries of women would be written on the wooden walls. "And you like this woman?"

"Yes." Garth folded his arms, nearly grinding the word out between his teeth. "She's…well, something happened to her."

"What happened to her?"

"I don't know." Garth wanted to know what had happened to Juliette, wanted to make sure it never happened again. He suspected her rejection of him had stemmed from fear over…he didn't know what, and that frustrated him as much as the termination of their relationship.

Pete sighed as he leaned against the railing separating the men from the horses. "Well, normally I'd say that when a woman tells you to stop coming around, you should stop coming around. But it sounds like you didn't do anything stupid to warrant that. So something else must've happened."

"Or something spooked her," Garth said. "Or she has issues from the past, or—"

"Yeah, yeah. We all got problems." Pete held up his hand. "I forced Chelsea to talk to me, and that backfired once, and then worked out for us." He clapped Garth on the shoulder as Paul returned. "That's all I got for you, Boss."

Garth let Pete's words bounce around in his brain as he walked to his cabin. He just needed two minutes with Juliette when she wasn't one second away from going nuclear or one breath away from crying.

The look on her face in the barn...the sorrow and grief had nearly broken his heart. How did she come to be so traumatized? He was smart enough to know her anger wasn't because of him. Or because she had to ride out to the herd to check them for pinkeye. No, something deeper existed there.

And Garth suddenly wanted to dig.

"JULIETTE, DON'T HANG UP," HE SAID WHEN SHE answered her phone. "I just wanted to make sure you got home okay."

"I got home okay." Her voice over the line sounded small and timid and beautiful. It soothed something in Garth's soul that hadn't been still since Kim died.

"Okay, great," he said. "Listen, I just—can you answer one question for me? Just one, I swear."

A moment too long passed before she said, "Okay."

"You asked me what I wanted from you. In the barn earlier. Remember?"

"Is that your one question?"

Garth smiled though panic raced through him. "No, that's not the question. I—" He cleared his throat. "I just want you to be happy. So I wanted to ask: What will make you happy?"

Silence echoed through the line, piling on top of itself until it was so thick, Garth couldn't break it with his voice.

"I have to go," Juliette said. "I'll see you in a couple of hours."

"Okay," Garth said. "Wait. What? Why will you see me in a couple of hours?"

"I'm coming out to inspect the herd. Didn't you talk to David?"

"I haven't seen David yet. Tell me yourself."

"Okay, *Boss*," she said, but she wore a smile in her tone. "I decided to come out on the range with you and inspect the herd. I just had to come get some clothes and supplies."

Garth reeled from the emotional whiplash. "You're coming back?"

"You don't have to sound so surprised."

"Actually, Juliette, I do. You ran from the ranch like it was going up into a tornado. You haven't spoken to me for months. Really *spoken* to me. I—" Garth cut himself off, unwilling to speak to her out of anger or frustration.

"You what?" she asked. "Finish that sentence, Garth."

He pictured the icy fire she'd have flashing in her blue eyes. He'd seen it before when she spoke with such a sharp tongue. He drummed up his courage and closed his eyes in a long blink. "I miss you," he said.

This silence buried him.

"Well, I—" she sputtered.

"You what?" he asked.

"You got your one question."

"You never answered it." Garth held his breath while he waited for her to hang up on him.

"I'm still trying to figure it out," she said. "I'll see you in a little while, okay?"

He'd barely said, "Okay," before she hung up. At least she'd finished the conversation this time.

CHAPTER FOUR

Sharp pain cut through Juliette's abdomen. She felt like her intestines had doubled their kinks, their twists and turns, until she was impossibly tangled up inside. She needed to speak to Garth. Really speak to him the way he wanted her to.

The very idea had her nauseous. Her fingers tightened around the steering wheel and she pressed her teeth together, reminding herself to keep her car aimed toward the ranch. She'd said she was coming back, and she wasn't a liar.

At least not to Garth. Or herself. The only person she'd lied to was Brad, and she'd had to. The situation warranted it, and she'd made her peace with the things she'd taken, the money she'd used, the fibs she'd told so she could find a better life for herself.

She rounded the administration trailer and pulled beside Garth's truck next to his cabin. She'd barely stepped from the car before he came trotting down his front steps. "You really came back."

She opened the backdoor and retrieved her pack. She shouldered it before facing him. "I hope you have a gentle horse for me. I'm not much for riding."

A grin split his face, and Juliette pocketed her hands so she wouldn't reach up and cradle his cheek in her palm, add her smile to his, and invite him down for a kiss.

She'd thought about kissing him twice in less than twelve hours, a fact that didn't escape her.

"You'll be fine." He gestured for her to come around the back of his house. "I sent a group ahead of us. They'll get the cabin set up and start to corral the sick cattle." He glanced at the sky. "We'll barely make it by nightfall, so you'll have to administer the drops to the cows tomorrow."

Juliette's skin felt like someone had dropped an electric web on it. Buzzing skated up her arms and sent a shiver down her back. "Where will I sleep?"

He cut her a quick glance. "In the cabin with us. It's large, and I asked Ethan to section off a cot for you so you can change or…whatever."

She swallowed against the rising panic. "How many men did you send ahead?"

"Four."

She had to sleep in a cabin with five men, one of which she wanted to kiss. Would she have any privacy? How many layers could she wear in this sweltering heat?

"The cabin's really big, Juliette. It has two bathrooms,

running water, the works." He checked the straps on the saddle, though she was sure he'd already secured them correctly. "Well, not the works. No AC."

Juliette's heart flipped for a different reason. "No AC?" That sounded worse than sharing a bathroom with five men.

He chuckled. "Lots of windows though. And it cools down at night."

"Great," she grumbled under her breath. She stepped over to a black and white horse, as she recognized the tall almost-burgundy mare as Garth's. She remembered the first time she'd seen him riding the horse. She'd thought he was the finest cowboy in all of Texas, and the feeling still remained.

His hand landed on hers as she reached for the saddle. A zing of pleasure shot through her body, untwisting the sickness in her guts, smoothing out the ragged places in her mind.

"Take your pack off first," he said, his breath drifting over her shoulder. "You'll never get up with that thing on."

She stepped back, reluctantly removed her hand from under his, and mutely slid off the backpack. Juliette thought about her canteen, sunscreen, the hat she'd packed as she stared at Garth. Anything to stop herself from kissing him.

He seemed equally transfixed with her, and even moved closer and slid one arm around her waist. She stiffened, though she had no desire to step out of his embrace.

Her breath came quicker. Her brain battled her heart harder.

"Garth." Her voice scratched her throat. "I—"

"Don't tell me to step back," he said, drawing her closer as his voice hushed. "I don't want to, and I don't think you really want me to."

He brought her so close, she had no choice but to lay her cheek against his chest. She listened to the steady clomping of his heart, stole strength from it. Salty tears formed in the corners of her eyes. She had so many secrets—from who she really was, to the fact that she was probably still married—and she didn't know how to unearth them. She'd kept them buried for so long. So long.

Too long.

"Juliette?" He shifted, and she reached up and clung to him like he could save her from an awful fate.

"There are things you don't know about me," she managed to say. Things she wanted to share with someone, if only to relieve the burden she'd carried alone for years. Things she specifically wanted to share with *him*.

"I want to know everything about you," he whispered, his lips lightly landing just behind her ear.

Sparks exploded from the contact, and she felt one breath away from abandoning all reason and giving him better access to her mouth. Her brain finally kicked in, warning her of what could happen if she kissed him.

She scrambled backward, meeting horseflesh and causing the animal to stutter-step. Juliette braced her hands against the mare's ribs. "What if you don't like what you learn?"

His eyes stormed, the familiar heat in them hotter than she'd ever seen. "Impossible," he said, his voice low enough to carry the bass line in the choir at church. "And I'll start. I've been married before. Two and a half years ago, my wife died from an aggressive pancreatic cancer."

Married before rang in her ears. Garth knew love. Had been in love. Relief that Juliette had only felt once—when she'd escaped from Brad—sang through her soul.

Trust him, came into her mind, but she had not thought it. Her brain and her heart agreed with the feeling, and she took a breath that burned like acid in her lungs.

"Tell me about her."

GARTH NEEDED TO STOP TALKING ALREADY. BUT speaking about Kim was easy, and it filled the sky, the miles, the time until they reached the first stream that crossed through the wide open range.

He pulled Ace to a stop, though the horse was itching to get to the water. He dismounted, finally able to get his vocal chords to go silent, and led the horse to the edge of the stream. Garth turned to help Juliette down and watched her slip to the ground in the most unladylike fashion possible. She stumbled away from Cupid, her forward momentum nearly taking her down to the dirt face-first.

Garth threw his head back and laughed. The sound flew into the sky, soared through his soul on its way out of his mouth. Ace tossed him a disdainful look, but Cupid startled and jostled a few steps away. The water distracted her, and she joined Ace at the stream while Juliette speared Garth with a daggered look.

He held up his hands in surrender, his chest still filled with chuckles. "I'm sorry. I am. That was just the funniest thing I've ever seen." He laughed again, seeing her fumble forward again in his mind's eye.

Before he knew it, she'd crossed the distance between them and planted one palm against his chest. Her touch burned, even through cloth, and he sobered instantly.

He watched her face as it broke into a smile—the first he'd seen her wear in months. At least the first he'd seen her wear *for him* in months.

"We aren't all blessed with grace," she said.

"Is that what I have?" he teased.

She moved away and grumbled something under her breath as she knelt upstream from the horses and filled her canteen. He collected his from his saddlebag and joined her.

"You know, I've been talking the whole time."

"Not true," she said. "I've asked questions and added stuff."

Her "stuff" had been things like, "You must have loved her," and "Why couldn't you stay in Montana?"

He'd answered everything she'd asked, and for the first time since Kim's death, Garth felt free. Still, something nagged at him. Something that told him not to push Juliette too hard or too fast. Something that told him he wouldn't be able to survive another rejection from her, especially not after everything he'd just told her about his first wife.

"So will I get to learn anything about you on this ride?" He stood and stretched his back. Juliette did the same, her eyes closed as she faced the sky. The golden evening light cast a hue of perfection on her tan skin, and Garth was struck dumb watching her.

She definitely had grace. Just not when it came to dismounting.

She straightened, turned her face into the setting sun, and smiled. "I used to live in Montana too."

Garth blinked, blinked against her declaration. "Really? Which part?" The state was huge, but somehow he hoped she'd lived somewhere near Missoula, where he'd buried Kim.

Shutters drew over her eyes and she hugged herself as if cold, though the summer temperatures had to be near ninety. "That's one of my secrets."

Her voice blew through him like an icy wind. His fingers curled into fists, and he worked to release them. "Why is where you lived a secret?"

"It just is."

"So I can't know?"

"If I tell you, you'll...." She stared at him, their gazes impossibly locked. He watched as panic paraded through her expression, as she shivered in the sunlight.

"I'll what?"

She shrugged as she stepped closer to him. "I don't know what, and that's what scares me."

He closed the distance between them and slid his hands up her arms. Gooseflesh popped out over her arms and shoulders and he tried to warm them away with friction. "Juliette, what happened to you?"

He didn't know where the question came from, only that it was there and he was certain something terrible had happened in Montana. She caved into his arms, hers nestled against his chest instead of snaking around him the way he'd like.

What should I do? he thought, sending the question to the heavens, pleading with the Lord to guide him when it came to Juliette. He didn't want to push her away, but he needed to know the details of her life if they were to be together.

And he wanted to spend a lot of together time with her.

"Hey, its okay," he said when he felt her tremble. "You'll tell me when you're ready." He released her though every cell in his body wanted to keep holding her. She remained as still as stone while he gathered their canteens and slid them into their packs.

"We better get going so we don't have to ride in the dark."

That got her moving—and another chuckle to lift through Garth's chest. *She just needs time*, he told himself, and the thought sounded good and true in his mind. *Just give her time.*

———

THEY DIDN'T SPEAK ABOUT ANYTHING important the rest of the way to the cabin. Meaningless things about someone on the ranch, or something Pastor Scott had said at church over the months. He told her a couple of stories of his childhood, and she shared one of her own. He noticed that she shared no specifics, didn't give any names of siblings, places, schools, nothing. When he asked where she'd gotten her veterinarian technician certificate, she'd said, "Montana."

So Garth had told her about his work on the Bluebonnet Ranch outside of Billings, and his years getting his business degree while he wrangled cattle and horses and men. He hardly used his degree, but it looked good on his resume, and he knew it had put him in the top spot when the job of foreman had come up at Three Rivers. Frank Ackerman had said so.

By the time the glittering lights of the cabin came into view, a headache assaulted the back of Garth's skull. "There it is."

"Thank goodness," Juliette sighed. "I was just about to slide off this beast, no matter if you laughed at me for the rest of my life."

Garth leaned over and took her reins from her fingers.

"I'll take those then. You just have to hold on for a few more minutes."

"This is the most my abs have worked in the past, well, forever."

"Now you know why cowboys have washboard abs." Garth chuckled until he felt the weight of her gaze on the side of his face. He met her stare, and though the twilight was thick between them, he saw a spark in her eyes. That spark leapt from her to him, and a tether formed between them.

Ace pulled against Garth's hold, anxious to get to the cabin, get everything off his back, and get his nose in a bag of oats. Garth tore his gaze from Juliette, a river of satisfaction singing through his bloodstream.

Ethan met them at the gate, taking the reins for both horses while Garth jumped lightly to the ground.

"Now you're just showing off," Juliette said with a teasing lilt in her voice and a tiny smile riding her lips.

He offered his hand to help her, and she took her time sliding her fingers into his. Garth half-hoped she'd fall into his arms and he could sweep her off her feet and carry her toward the cabin.

But she dismounted smoothly with barely any help. "See? Easy," he said.

"Let's hope this takes a couple of days," she said, giving Cupid the evil eye as Ethan led her and Ace toward the barn. "I don't think I can ride a horse for a while."

Garth didn't tell her she'd have to ride out to the herd, that this was just the cabin where the men stayed, not the pen where they corralled the cattle. She needed to wash and eat and sleep before she learned that.

"Food back here, Boss," one of the boys called, and Garth tucked Juliette's hand into his elbow as they started across the field.

"Something smells good," Juliette said.

"Not as good as what you cook." Garth hoped she'd invite him over after church this upcoming Sunday, but she simply nudged him with her shoulder and smiled at the ground.

Garth paused as they approached the back door of the cabin. "Bathroom's in there. You can go on and wash up. Come on out and eat when you're ready." He nodded toward the fire, where three men loitered around the flames.

She gazed up at him, her eyes unreadable. "Thank you," she murmured just before pushing onto her toes and pressing a kiss to his cheek. Heat flooded his body, stemming from where her lips had lingered.

She slipped away from him and through the door, and still Garth remained frozen.

Hours later, after everyone had had their fill of baked beans and burgers, after the horses had been attended to, after everyone had gone to bed, Garth lay on the cot nearest the door. Awake. Staring at the ceiling. Thinking about Juliette and her kiss that had missed its mark.

Unable to be confined by walls any longer, he silently sat up and stole out the exit. Outside, the stars seemed to wink down on him, reminding him of how great and grand the universe was and how small and insignificant he was. At the same time, he knew there was a Higher Being who cared about him, even if Garth himself wasn't the biggest and best of His creations.

He'd always known it, from the time he sat next to his mother as she read him stories from the Bible. Whenever he wasn't sure what decision to make, or what to do, he thought of her. Of her unwavering faith. Of her absolute love.

He'd lost her too early too, but his memories of her contained nothing but happiness. He smiled at the stars as he strolled around the perimeter of the fence. If only life could be as easy as enjoying a summer night sky stuffed full of stars, as refreshing as taking a deep breath of country air, as joyful as listening to a horse snuffle in the dark.

Garth stopped and leaned against a fence post, staring into the dark distance. Minutes ticked by as he thought about his wife, about all he'd said about her to Juliette. This time, though, he didn't feel the usual ache in his soul. He didn't feel plagued by unrelenting sadness.

This time, from sharing her life with someone else, he'd found a way to let her go.

CHAPTER FIVE

*J*uliette couldn't sleep. The breathing bodies on the other side of the curtain kept her awake. She got up and moved to the window, startling when she sensed movement just out of her sight. She strained to see against the dark, finally making out a figure standing at the fence.

The man turned his head and Juliette recognized his strong profile with its sloped nose and square jaw. Garth.

Quickly, and without thinking, she stuffed her feet into her boots and tread as quietly as she could to the exit. Once free of the cabin, she moved quicker, not bothering to lighten her steps.

Still, Garth did not turn toward her as she neared him. "Garth?"

He finally moved, twitching his head slightly toward the cabin. "Can't sleep, Juliette?"

She joined him at the fence and leaned her elbows on it

the way he did. "It's too quiet out here. And too noisy at the same time."

Garth reached over and covered her hand with his. Easy, and slow, and careful, giving her an opportunity to pull away or reprimand him. She did neither. She relaxed into his side, tired of fighting a losing battle.

"Yeah, men can cause a ruckus at night."

Juliette took a deep breath, bracing herself for an unknown reaction. "My husband was as quiet as a mouse." Every muscle stretched tight; her fingers clamped down on Garth's.

"You were married?" he asked in a low voice, almost a growl.

"Yes," she said, her voice going numb, much the same way it used to when Brad would yell at her and demand answers. She'd learned to speak with as little emotion as possible so as to not rile him further. "He was…." She took a shuddering breath. "He was not a nice man." She cleared her throat and almost choked. "I—I—"

Garth turned toward her, his expression open and curious, his arm lifting to settle around her shoulders, bringing her closer to him, closer to being comfortable. "You what?"

"I left him," Juliette blurted, the rest of the words pulsing against the back of her tongue. "He—he hurt me, and I took it, and then one day, I couldn't take it anymore, and I left. I left and I never went back. I left, and I'm never *going* back." Her chin shook though she tried to tame it.

She felt shattered inside, with pointed pieces that cut and sliced and hurt.

"Hey, okay." Garth gathered her fully into his arms and stroked her hair. "You don't have to go back. No one's going to make you go back."

Juliette enjoyed the warmth from Garth's body, the careful way he touched her, and the soothing quality of his voice. She pulled back slightly and looked up at him. "Garth?"

"Hmm?"

She didn't know what to say. She swept her fingers through his salt-and-pepper hair, drawing his head down, bringing his mouth closer to hers. He didn't seem to understand her meaning, or he wanted her to be the one who committed fully first. She stretched up and touched her lips to his, expecting sparks and pins and needles.

She got an explosion. Once the heat faded to a level she could think through, she felt tenderness and adoration in Garth's touch she'd never experienced before. With Garth's passion and compassion, she realized that she was worth loving, and that she was ready to let someone love her.

She broke the contact and stepped back, her heart warring against her ribcage. "I'm—I'm sorry. I don't know—"

"You're apologizing for kissing me?" He put himself where she'd just been, but because he took up more room than her, he could embrace her again if he chose to. He kept his hands at his sides as he looked at her.

She squirmed under the honesty of his gaze. "No."

A slow smile cracked his serious façade. "Okay, then."

"All right." Warmth spread through her, eliminating all pockets of cold. A grin pulled at her lips.

"Well, we better get back to the cabin." Noise ground through his throat. "Wouldn't want anyone to get the wrong idea about us."

Juliette walked beside him, lightening her steps as they entered the cabin. She continued past the men and behind her curtain, where she settled back on her cot. She stared at the ceiling, that goofy grin still stuck in place.

She hadn't told him everything, but she'd started and it felt so, so good to get the words out. The ones she still had to say swirled inside like poison. She pushed away what still needed to be done in favor of focusing on the kiss that had changed her reality.

You're in deep now, her rational side whispered.

Yeah, her heart tapped out. *And it feels good.*

MORNING ON THE RANGE CAME AT AN HOUR THAT Juliette hadn't seen for a long time. But she couldn't sleep with all the boots, all the male voices speaking in froggy tones. So she got up and pulled on fresh jeans and a blue tank top. She slid her arms into her white technician jacket with a dog embroidered on the pocket as she pulled the curtain back.

The cowboys stilled as she emerged, threading trepidation through her. They'd been polite last night as they served her dinner and made light conversation. But now, she felt like they'd never seen a woman before.

"Morning, boys," she said, glancing past them to locate Garth, but he wasn't in the cabin. "What's the plan?"

They'd pulled their cots into a rough circle and held cards. Ethan threw one on the pile on the floor between them. "Boss went to check the herd. Said to hang tight until he came back."

Juliette half wished he'd woken her to go with him, while the other part of her was eternally grateful she hadn't had to get on another horse so soon.

"So this is hanging tight?"

"Ain't nothin' else to do." Ethan shot her a glance. "You wanna play?"

She strode toward them. "Sure. Can I sit with you, Kenny?"

Kenny made room for her on the end of his cot and Ethan dealt her in, explaining the rules of the two-card poker as he did. She watched each man as they played and noticed how Ethan's eyes flickered around the group when he had good cards and how he studied the floor when he didn't.

Aaron never looked up from his cards unless they were good, almost like he'd been caught doing something he shouldn't and he wanted to check and make sure no one else knew. Kenny was as easy to read as a book, with frowns and grins and sighs. Charlie was the hardest to figure out, and Juliette tried to mimic him.

"Call," he said, sliding her a glare out of his slitted eyes. "I know you ain't got nothin' good."

"How do you know?" she asked.

He threw his cards down. "'Cause I don't."

She burst out laughing as she threw her pitiful cards down. "I'm that easy to read, huh?"

"Not bad." Charlie chuckled too, his mustache bouncing with the sound.

"I hate to interrupt," Garth said from behind Charlie. Juliette lifted her eyes to the doorway, where Garth leaned, a sly smile on his face. "But it's time to head out. It'll take all of us." He waved for them to follow him as he stepped back outside. "Saddle up, boys."

Juliette stifled a whimper as she rose to go with the cowboys. She hurried ahead to catch Garth. "How far is it?"

His arm flinched toward her, but he pulled it back to his side. "Only about a mile." He slowed his step and peered at her. "Think you can make it?"

Juliette wanted to get lost in the depths of his thundercloud eyes and sink into his kiss again. Instead, she nodded. "A mile sounds doable. Let me get my medical bag."

By the time she'd gone back to the cabin to get the supplies and made it to the barn, everyone had their horses saddled and ready to go. Ethan rode his black stallion toward the gate and then turned back.

"Up you go." Garth took her medical bag in one hand and directed her toward Cupid with the other. Juliette used his steadiness to push herself up and she landed in the saddle with a grunt of pain. She wasn't ready to be on horseback again and every bone in her body testified of it—especially her tailbone.

"Maybe I could walk the mile," she said, trying not to whimper at the way her thighs chafed against the saddle.

Garth shouldered her bag and handed over her hat before he mounted his horse. "Nope. You're already on." He whistled. "Let's go, boys."

Juliette expected him to ride out front with his cowboys, but he didn't. And the other wranglers didn't clump together so they could gossip about the card game or last night's dinner. They spread out on the range, each cowboy claiming his own piece of the wilderness.

Garth settled next to her, the same way he had last night, and they brought up the rear of the group. He nudged his horse closer and held out his hand for her to hold. Giddiness galloped through her and she placed her palm against his.

"Did you get any sleep?" he asked, and the tender tone tore through Juliette's fleshy heart.

"Yeah." She sounded slightly strangled. "Those cots aren't half-bad. How'd you sleep?"

"Not great." He squeezed her hand. "I kept thinking about that kiss."

She found a slight curve in those lips she'd kissed last night, and suddenly that was all she could think about too.

"Garth," she started. "I have something else to tell you."

"Shoot."

Cupid plodded along for a few strides before she found her voice. "When I said I left my husband, I meant it literally." She dug around in her saddlebag for her sunglasses. She couldn't find them, couldn't hide her eyes. At least out here, no one could overhear. "I ran away, did the whole disguise thing, no using credit cards, assumed a new identity, all of that."

Garth didn't speak. He didn't look at her either.

Nervous energy filled her stomach and surged upward, choking her. "Say something."

"I don't know what to say." He finally swung his gaze her way. "I hate that you were hurt. You don't deserve that."

"No one does," ghosted between her lips. He wasn't going to probe for more information about her escape? He didn't need to know how Brad had hurt her so badly that she'd been forced to run away?

"Where did you live, Juliette?"

The question she'd dreaded answering. Because once she told him, he'd put the pieces together. All of them. And he seemed to know it. Of all the questions he could've asked, he'd chosen that one.

"Bozeman." She angled her head away from him so she couldn't see his reaction. She didn't need to look at him to practically hear the gears turning in his head.

"Juli Thornton," he murmured.

Pain and panic and pure adrenaline rushed through her. "Don't."

"You were married to Brad Thornton, the rodeo champion." Garth pulled his horse to a stop, and Cupid automatically copied Ace. She wanted to spur Cupid into a gallop, a full-out run, so she could get away from this conversation.

"Am I right?" he asked.

She nodded, her throat too clogged to speak.

"I knew him," Garth said. "I mean, I *know* him. We're still in touch online." His jaw hardened and his eyes sparked with angry fire. "I want to hurt him, Juliette. I had no idea he'd abused you. He never brought you anywhere. We never went to his house. You have to know I didn't—"

She held up her hand. "I know. And anyway, he was very careful about placing his punches. Even if you had met me, you wouldn't have known."

Garth recoiled as if she'd landed a right hook to his jawbone. He recovered and brought both of his hands down to cover hers. "I'm so sorry."

She pressed back tears. "That's not the worst of it, Garth."

He swallowed, obviously bracing himself for whatever she had to say.

"We might still be married." Juliette delivered the words with precision, without emotion.

"What?"

"I never filed for divorce." Desperation and embarrassment flooded her now, loosening her tongue. "I couldn't. I was on the run, moving all the time, trying to make sure he could never find me. If I filed for divorce, he'd know where I was. I'd have to go to court. I couldn't risk that."

Garth blinked at her. "Surely he filed for divorce. His wife—" He cut himself off and glanced away. "You left a long time ago. What? Gotta be almost ten years."

"If he filed, I don't know about it. Which is just fine with me. It means he doesn't know where I am, doesn't know where to send the papers. In Montana, the other party has ninety days to contest or show up in court. If they don't, the judge can issue a divorce without them."

"Then surely he did that."

Juliette wasn't sure. She wouldn't put it past Brad to keep their marriage intact simply to exert his control over her in whatever small way he could. He wouldn't need to marry another woman to exert control over her, dominate her, hurt her.

"I mean, he's got to have found someone else by now."

She grimaced just thinking about him hitting another woman. "I hope not," she said. "You lived in Montana until a couple of years ago. You're friends with him on social media. You should be able to find out."

She absolutely refused to use social media, and she never checked Brad's. With his resources, he could find out who was looking at his profiles. She'd done everything the anonymous chatline for abused women had told her, and that included staying off the computer and stuffing away her curiosity about Brad's life.

She didn't care what his life was like, but it would be

nice to know if he'd moved on, if maybe she could relax her constant worries. She couldn't believe how close to Brad she'd gotten. Sure, he was two thousand miles away, in another state. He didn't know where she lived. But there was only one degree of separation between him and Garth—and now Juliette.

Stupid, she chastised herself. She should've listened to her brain and not her heart. She gently pulled her hands out from under Garth's, contemplating her next move. She hadn't been to New England yet, and she'd heard the fall leaves in Maine were a sight to behold.

Garth got his horse moving again, the slow rhythm of the hooves a complete opposite to his racing thoughts.

Juliette Thompson, the woman he felt himself falling in love with, had been married to an old ranch friend. And old ranch friend who'd turned into a rodeo champion. A rodeo champion who beat his wife. His wife who was Juliette Thompson, who Garth wanted to spend a lot more time with—and maybe make *his* wife.

Garth felt like throwing up. He felt like racing back to Three Rivers, hopping on a plane, and flying straight to Montana so he could give Brad a taste of his own medicine. He recoiled from the vengeful thoughts. He wasn't a violent person, and though Brad deserved a beating—and worse—Garth wouldn't be the one to mete it out to him.

God would take care of Brad, and Garth knew that punishment would be worse than anything he could do.

"Say something," Juliette begged again. "I hate this silence."

Truth was, Garth wasn't sure what to say. How could he reassure her? What could he possibly tell her to help her?

"We'll figure it out," he said, not quite sure what he meant. "I'll find out if he's with someone else, if he's divorced. If he is, that's that."

Juliette shook her head, sending a single tear flying. She wiped her face. "With Brad, nothing is ever over. He always said he'd kill me if I left him. I believe he still would, if he knew where I was."

Everything fell into place all at once with a deafening clang inside Garth's brain. "That's why you broke things off in April. You found out I'd been friends with him."

"Yes." She sounded so small, so hurt.

Garth wanted to wrap his arms around her and protect her from everything and everyone. A new ache started in his chest, one that yearned to provide a refuge for her.

"I thought it too big of a risk for us to…you know. Have a relationship. I mean, you wouldn't be able to post any pictures of us together."

Frustration pooled beneath his tongue. "So why'd you kiss me last night?" He watched her, trying to get a read on her.

She fidgeted in her seat, held her reins too tight. "Because I wanted to. It felt so good to finally tell someone something real about myself, about who I really am." She met his gaze with pleading in hers. "I don't like that he's still dictating my life. I like you, and I wanted to kiss you, and so I did."

She liked him. She wanted to kiss him. New determination filled him. "We'll figure everything out." He reached for her hand again, beyond glad when she gave it to him to hold. He brought her knuckles to his lips and kissed them. "Okay? I'll help you figure everything out."

CHAPTER SIX

*J*uliette's stomach writhed with another truth that wanted to come out. "Garth, I've been in Three Rivers for three years. It's time for me to move on."

"No."

"It's not safe to stay in one place for so long."

"You're not moving."

"You don't get to—"

"Juliette, please." The undertones of desperation shut down her argument. "Let me look into a few things before you pack up and run away." He squeezed her fingers. "Please?"

She pressed her lips together and nodded. "Okay."

They plodded along in companionable silence for a few minutes. Juliette wasn't sure why she suddenly felt the need to leave. Or why it had felt so right and so good to kiss Garth if she was going to move the second she returned to town. She cast her eyes to the morning skies and sent up a prayer for guidance, for strength, for clear eyes to see what she should do.

"Why'd you come here?" Garth asked, breaking the reverie she'd fallen into.

Juliette searched for the real reason, wanting to be authentic and true to herself. Especially since she didn't need to hide anything from Garth anymore. "Tom lived here. I knew Brad wouldn't look for me in the same place as a family member."

"Tom doesn't live here anymore."

"Exactly why I shouldn't be living here anymore either."

"But you can't go back to Montana."

"No." Juliette's patience began to wear thin. Someone who hadn't lived the last decade of their life on the run would never understand. Someone who hadn't changed their hair color more times than they could count, who hadn't worried about using credit cards and filing taxes or leaving any sort of trail just couldn't get it.

"But I can go anywhere else I want. Listen, it's like when you're lost. You stay put and wait for help, right? Because someone will find you. It's best to keep moving if you want to stay lost. And, Garth, I don't want to be found."

He exhaled angrily. "I don't want you to leave."

She didn't want to leave either, and her rational side told her to *slow down, assess everything before moving.* "Let's see what you can figure out. Then, if I need to leave, I leave. I won't put you in danger."

He scoffed. "I can handle Brad Thornton." His fingers flexed like he'd like to meet him right now and make pizza out of his face.

"You have no idea what he's capable of."

Garth's shoulders drooped and the jumping muscle in his jaw quieted. "You're right. I'm so sorry I don't know what he's capable of. I'm even angrier that you do." He kissed her knuckles again and released her hand. She mourned the loss, wishing he could remain by her side indefinitely.

They arrived at the corral, and she managed to get off Cupid without embarrassing herself. She stared at the black sea of cattle, wondering how long it would take to check them all and administer the eye drops they needed. Days, maybe. Each infected cow would need to be treated multiple times.

Her heart skipped a beat when she realized she may not have brought enough medicine. She couldn't repeat the horseback ride out to this remote corner of the ranch. The very thought made tears spring to her eyes.

"Ethan and the other boys'll get 'em lined up." Garth gestured for her to follow him. "We'll be back here, checking them as they come through the chutes."

Juliette went with him through the barn to a large corral behind it. An impossible maze of fence lines stretched before her. Garth moved through them with strength and confidence, the same way he did everything.

She followed the best she could with her oversized medical bag perched on her back. He finally climbed a set of stairs in the middle of the arena and indicated that she should go up the second set.

Once on the platform, she realized the method to the madness. It especially helped when Ethan opened the gate and a single cow was allowed into the area. Then Juliette could see the lines, see how the cattle would be lined up and herded toward her and Garth, where they could check for the infection and administer medicine.

And so the hours passed. Sometimes the cows weren't too appreciative of someone getting right in their faces. Garth was always there to help, stepping over the space between them and wrestling the cow into submission. Juliette enjoyed watching him work, the way his muscles bunched, the way he never got riled up, only focused on the task to be completed.

His calm energy seeped into her as they inspected the entire herd. The cattle had moved through the chutes to a fenced field beyond, completely content with their new pasture.

By the position of the sun and the grumbling in her stomach, Juliette anticipated that it was just past lunchtime.

"Now what, Doc?" Garth asked.

Juliette resisted the urge to correct him. "We do it all again just before dinner time." She wiped a grimy hand across her forehead, already tired.

"So we can eat and get some shut eye now, right?" He

stepped down his ladder and started to move back to the barn.

She laughed as she followed him. "If that's what you want, Mister Foreman."

He spun back to her, sweeping one hand around her waist and one across the side of her face to move her hair out of the way. "What I want, Juliette, is this." He touched his lips to hers, creating a ball of heat that expanded up her throat with the passion and gentle insistence of his lips against hers. In the safety of his arms, with the smell of him in her nose, and the pressure of his mouth against hers, she believed—maybe for the first time—that she could be happy again.

That she could have a real life again. That she could leave Brad in the past and just be herself again.

Two days later, the cattle had been treated five times. "That should be enough," Juliette told Garth. "I'm out of clothes, and I haven't showered for days, and I need to get back to the clinic." Running water at the cabin meant a sink and a toilet, not a shower. When Juliette had found out, all five men had assured her she smelled the best out of the bunch.

She held up her hand as Garth started to speak. "I know, I know. You told David we'd be gone for a few days. You said I don't smell." She smiled at him, inviting him to come closer and kiss her, the way he'd been doing anytime the chance presented itself over the past forty-eight hours.

He seemed to be able to read her mind, because he stepped across the divide and onto her platform, his hands finding their place on her waist, his lips tracing a line from her ear to her mouth. "You don't smell that bad to me."

"That bad?" She pulled away. He hadn't showered for days either, but she liked the woodsy smell of him. The way he took on the scent of the range, with its fresh air and open feeling.

He smiled and pressed his lips to hers in response. She didn't feel a twinge of guilt about kissing Garth, though she might still be married. Brad had broken his vows only two days into their marriage, and Juliette had to believe she was allowed to find happiness again.

It'll work out, she'd told herself over the past few days. Before she could deepen the kiss and really lose herself in his touch, Ethan called to them from the barn. "Time to head back if we want to get to the ranch by dinnertime."

Garth pulled away, but he didn't release her from his embrace. "Think you can ride all the way home?"

"Do I have a choice?"

Garth chuckled and kissed her forehead. "Not really."

It took a couple of hours to get back to the cabin, get it cleaned, and load everything up for the ride home. Again, the wranglers spread out on the range, each man in his own thoughts as they made for Three Rivers Ranch.

Juliette appreciated the silence, the time to be inside her head and really figure things out. With every stride of the horse, an uncomfortable sensation grew in her stomach. She'd been gone from her reality for days, and she wasn't sure she'd be able to maintain the fairy tale she and Garth had started once she returned to her regular life.

She wanted to. One glance at the confident, handsome, caring cowboy, and oh, she wanted to keep living this fantasy.

But she had a feeling the façade of happiness would crack once they returned. Her heart grew heavy as they got closer and closer. And by the time she slid from Cupid's back, not only did pain radiate from her back, legs, and behind, but from her heart too.

Garth had enjoyed his time out on the range immensely. More than he had any other time he'd ridden out to the north cabin, more than any other time he'd had to go out and tag cattle, or attend to cattle, or any of the various jobs he'd done on the ranches he'd worked.

He knew it was because of Juliette. He'd never kissed a beautiful woman at midnight, or on the platform of a chute, or pressed up against the side of the cabin while four other men slept. He'd never held a pretty lady's hand next to a fire while their tin foil dinners baked, or made up an excuse to get her over to the horse barn so he could kiss her so completely he wasn't sure how he could function without her.

His mind had not fallen back to Kim the way it usually did. Before she died, she'd made him promise to find someone else to love, and Garth had vowed he would. Kim lived on the ranch with him, but she wasn't overly fond of animals, and never came out on the range, never rode a horse, and preferred the gas fireplace to a real wood-burning one. Garth had loved that she was different from him, but also appreciated that he and Juliette had a little more in common.

"I'll come out on...." Juliette's brow furrowed as she looked over his shoulder toward the administration building. "What day is today? Wednesday?"

Garth nodded and leaned into the side of his cabin. "Yep. Only Wednesday." The shade felt glorious after so many hours under the sun.

"I feel like I've lost a week," she said. "So I guess I'll come out on Friday after work, since I don't work weekends." She gave him a pointed glare that held more heat than anger. "See how those bulls are doing."

"Thanks, Juliette." He flashed her a smile, satisfied when a blush crept into her face. "I'm sending a couple of boys out to the pasture up north to keep an eye on the herd we just medicated."

"They should be fine, but let me know if they're not." Her feet shuffled in the direction of her car, but she didn't actually step that way. She ducked her head and inched closer to him. Her actions set a fire beneath his blood, and he traced his fingertips up her arm, across her bare shoulder, to the back of her neck.

"'Bye." He leaned down and placed a chaste peck on her lips, pulling back before the kiss could really take root.

She rolled her eyes. "That's not a good-bye kiss."

Garth couldn't contain the grin on his face, though a bucket of fear iced his insides. Was she saying good-bye for now? Or good-bye for good?

He shelved his reservations, his fears. He'd take things one step at a time. "You want me to kiss you good-bye?"

She pressed into him, her palms against his chest, her head tilted back. "Yes."

He obliged, beyond happy to do so. He wanted Juliette to feel cherished, cared for, loved. As he kissed her good-bye, he realized he loved her. He broke the contact and leaned his forehead against hers, stunned by the strength of his feelings.

He knew he didn't love her as deeply as he'd loved Kim. He wondered if he even could. But he knew what love felt like, and he knew on some level—maybe the introductory level—he loved Juliette.

"That was better," she whispered, clinging to him for one last moment before turning, stooping to pick up her bags, and heading for her car.

Garth had a ranch to-do list a mile long, but it could wait. He retrieved his keys from his cabin and got in his truck, intending to follow Juliette home to make sure everything there was all right. Evening had started to come on just as they'd made it back to the ranch, and he wanted to ensure she got home safely.

He didn't follow at a creepy stalker distance but simply

drove into town like he was picking up groceries. Juliette had made a stop somewhere, because when Garth pulled onto the corner at the end of Sixth Street, her house sat in the twilight, the carport empty.

He adjusted the volume on the radio and settled into his seat to wait. Twenty minutes later, she drove past his truck without looking at it and pulled into her driveway. She parked and entered the house, disappearing from his sight.

A light snapped on in one of her front windows, which Garth knew from his previous dinner invitations at her house was the living room. Not two breaths later, the light went out.

Unease snaked through Garth's stomach. It was dark enough to warrant lights. Why had Juliette turned it off?

A car skidded around the corner behind him, nearly fishtailing into his truck, before rushing into Juliette's driveway. The driver parked the car at an angle—eliminating Juliette's ability to get out of the carport—and jumped from the car.

Though Garth hadn't seen Brad in several years, he recognized the celebrity rodeo rider easily enough. The tall build, the boxy face, the chestnut hair.

Adrenaline pulsed through his veins as Brad rushed into the house. Garth's stomach tightened; his mind buzzed; his throat dried out. He pulled out his phone and dialed 911. He needed to secure the situation. He needed backup—needed proof—against Brad.

After giving the operator Juliette's address and saying

someone had broken in, he jammed his truck into drive and swung behind Brad's rental car. He killed the engine and opened the door. Paused. Waited. Listened.

He couldn't hear anything beyond the normal neighborhood sounds. The door leading into the house stood open, as if someone had entered in a hurry. He stepped out of the truck and toward the door. Careful steps on the stairs kept his boots silent. He pressed into the wall and peered around the doorframe and into the house.

Brad hadn't turned the light on either, and Garth couldn't see anything. He heard a scuffling sound and one of Juliette's dogs whined. Then a scream cut through the dusky silence, sending all of Garth's nerves into a frenzy.

A yell followed the scream, along with a heavy thud, like the sound of a body hitting the floor, hard.

Garth swallowed, finding his tongue too thick. He swiped his palm against the wall, searching for the light switch. His fingers tripped over it, flipping the electricity on.

He stood in the doorway leading from the garage, with the kitchen in front of him, the living room to his left, and a small dining table beyond the kitchen. A doorway led to the right, through a laundry room toward the backyard, and a narrow hall would take him farther into the house to the bedrooms and bathrooms.

He didn't move a muscle, not even a twitch. Every cupboard in the kitchen had been emptied. Every item on the shelves in the living room tossed to the floor. The two chairs at the dining room table lay on their sides.

Amid all the chaos, on the mirror hanging on the far wall near the front entrance of the house, Garth saw words written in thick, black letters.

I found you.

A chill skated down his back, and he fumbled with the light switch until the room went dark. He'd seen enough to be able to navigate to the hall, where he suspected Brad had followed Juliette.

The sound of someone crying echoed toward him the closer he crept to the hall, and Garth flexed and released his fingers to keep himself grounded and calm.

"...thought I'd never find you!" Brad's enraged voice urged Garth to move faster, as did the sound of ripping cloth and another wail from Juliette. The fire that burned in Garth now spoke of fury.

"If you didn't want me to find you, you shouldn't have gone to your nephew's wedding." The loathing in Brad's voice made Garth's skin crawl. "You think I don't have friends everywhere?"

Garth caught movement through the crack of the door directly in front of him, and nudged it open with a fist. Brad stood with his back to the door, looming over the prostrate form of Juliette.

He reared his leg back as if to kick her as nasty words spewed from his mouth, and Garth could only see red. He charged forward, unwilling to watch the woman he loved get hurt. He collided with Brad in a tangle of limbs, and they landed in a heap on top of Juliette.

Garth rolled, shoving Brad toward the wall so Juliette

could move out from underneath him, their eyes meeting for one terrible moment. Blood wept from her nose and angry red welts marked her face. She continued under her bed with a groan and obvious pain etched in the set of her mouth. Garth returned his attention to Brad, who leaned against the wall, panting, his eyes manic and his breathing feverish.

"I've already called the cops," Garth said, pulling his leg out from under Brad's and standing. The man howled in pain, causing Garth to examine the angle of Brad's leg. It was bent oddly—certainly not the way knees should bend.

"You won't be able to kick anyone with that leg again."

"I'll kill you," Brad said between ragged breaths. "You've ruined...my rodeo ca-career. I'm worth —millions."

Garth laughed, a dark, loathsome sound he didn't know his body could make. He sensed movement behind him and caught Juliette's silhouette as she slipped out of the room and down the hall.

"Son, you're not worth anything." He looked down on Brad—a solidly built, muscular man—and wondered why someone like him needed to beat his wife.

He turned away and moved out of Brad's reach, happy the other man hadn't recognized him yet. "Did you file for divorce?"

Brad snarled, spat out some choice words, but didn't answer the question.

"That's fine," Garth said in the placating tone he used with horses. "There are other ways to find out."

He heard movement behind him, a grunt and a yelp of pain, but before he could move, a strong grip yanked on his ankle. He went down to one knee and pushed all his strength into both palms as they shot toward Brad's face.

Warm blood spurted over his hands from Brad's nose, and Garth scrambled away from him just as two officers entered the bedroom, weapons drawn. "Which one of you is Garth Ahlstrom?" one of them demanded.

"I am." Garth used the bed behind him to get to his feet as Brad exclaimed, "Garth?"

Garth ignored him. He straightened his shirt and found splatters of blood on it.

"Show me your ID," the second officer said.

Garth dug in his back pocket and produced his wallet. The officer kept his gun up until he examined the driver's license.

"And you are?" he asked Brad.

Brad remained silent, so Garth spoke for him. "That's the man who broke into the house and ransacked it. His name's Brad Thornton. He's Juliette Thompson's ex-husband."

The officers trained their weapons on Brad, who'd started squirming. "Stay still, sir. The paramedics will be here soon." One glanced at Garth and then nodded down the hall. "There are two officers in the garage with Miss Thompson. She's asking about you."

"I'm free to go?"

"To the garage."

Garth left Brad without a backward glance, wondering if Juliette would ever be able to do the same.

Before he stepped into the garage, he braced himself for what he'd find. He'd already seen Juliette bleeding. She had been able to get out of the house, so she couldn't be too badly broken. He hoped.

He took a deep breath and closed his eyes. He wanted to say a prayer, but he didn't even know what to ask for. His thoughts seemed to circle around each other, and he couldn't put one together.

Garth moved into the garage slowly, cautiously, looking for Juliette. He found the two officers near the back bumper of her car, shielding her from the small crowd of neighbors that had gathered on the sidewalk. Four cop cars cordoned off the street, red and blue lights flashing.

She leaned against the car like she couldn't stand by herself. Her right arm cradled her side in a new way, and Garth's heartstrings sounded a loud note. He hurried over to her, lightly touching her shoulder as he examined her.

Her nose had stopped bleeding, but the evidence of the injury still lingered on her face. Her skin was blotchy, and tears filed over her cheeks like soldiers.

"Juliette." He didn't dare gather her into his arms, especially with the way she wouldn't put weight on her left leg. "When will the ambulance arrive?" he asked the officers.

One tilted his head. "I can hear the sirens now."

Sure enough, Garth heard the wail of the emergency

vehicle as it came closer. "I'm riding with you," he said to Juliette, leaning down and placing a gentle kiss to her temple.

She nodded and her jaw worked like she was trying to be brave or trying to say something. He wasn't sure which.

"You want to press charges, ma'am?" one officer asked.

"Yes," Juliette said decisively. She glanced at Garth. "Will he go to jail?"

"I can't speak to that," the officer said. "But we'll make sure he's under guard at the hospital, and you won't be bothered."

"I need a restraining order," she said, but Garth could hardly hear it.

"I'll help you with that," Garth said. "Do you have an overnight bag or anything I can grab and bring with us?"

She watched as the ambulance pulled behind the police cars, then she turned toward him as if underwater. "I have a bag in the front hall closet. It's a dark red backpack. That'll have everything I need for now."

The EMTs arrived and asked Juliette what hurt the most. She indicated her ribs, and Garth finally noticed how shallow her breathing was. She mentioned her leg and how she couldn't put much weight on it, and Garth turned away.

The front door was locked, so he retraced his steps back to the garage entrance. He paused on the threshold and took in the devastation. Juliette would never come back here, he was certain of that. Even if he got her comfortable at the hospital and came back here and cleaned up, she wouldn't stay here. He didn't *want* her to stay here.

In Three Rivers, yes. But with him out at the ranch. Permanently.

As he stepped over picture frames and couch cushions toward the front hall closet, he knew he was deluding himself. She'd leave town—leave him—and find somewhere to start over. Maybe now she actually could, now that Brad could be removed from her life completely.

Garth wanted that safety for her. He just wanted it here.

Heaving a sigh, he collected the backpack and unlocked the front door to leave.

CHAPTER SEVEN

*J*uliette let the tears fall once she was away from the officers, away from the crowd that had come to see what had happened. She wasn't alone—Garth and a single EMT rode with her—but this was as private as she could get right now.

Garth noticed her tears and collected her left hand in both of his. "Don't cry," he said, his voice deep and comforting. "It's all okay now."

She shook her head, but couldn't vocalize that if Brad was still alive, nothing was okay. She felt numb on the inside, like maybe she'd swallowed dry ice and the cold smoke had spread through her body. She answered questions from doctors or nurses. She let them stick needles in her and take her temperature and wheel her into the x-ray room.

When she couldn't speak for herself, Garth did. When her eyes drifted closed from exhaustion, Garth reminded her to stay awake. When she needed to be moved, Garth pushed her wheelchair.

Finally, after a diagnosis of two broken ribs, a severely sprained ankle—but no break—and facial bruising—but no concussion—a nurse wearing pink scrubs helped Juliette into a hospital bed. It wasn't the nicest bed she'd ever slept in, but at the moment, it was the most wonderful. "Thank you," she managed to say and the nurse snapped off the lights as she left.

Only Garth remained at her side. He clutched her hand in his and touched his lips to her knuckles. She wanted to ask him why he'd been at her house, but the painkillers and extreme exhaustion weighed down her vocal chords and her eyelids, and she drifted into a medicated sleep.

WHEN SHE WOKE, SHE WAS ALONE. THE RELATIVE silence of the hospital brought her the same relief she'd always felt when it was quiet. Her mind traveled back through all the beatings, all of Brad's brutality. When she'd discovered her house in complete chaos and those terror-inducing words written on her mirror, she'd hurried to the bedroom to get the wad of cash from her nightstand drawer. She'd planned to grab the backpack from the front closet and set her sights on New England. Her heart had tore and bled when she thought of Garth, and that was the distraction Brad needed to sneak up on her.

She forced the fresh memory away and glanced around for Garth. He wasn't there. The first light of morning streamed through her window, so she shouldn't be surprised that Garth had left. But she was. Disappointed too.

The door opened a crack and he slipped in, carrying two travel mugs of coffee. "Hey, you're awake."

She tried to adjust herself to a more seated position, but hot pain screamed down her right side where Brad had kicked her twice with those steel-toed boots.

"Don't move," he said, setting the coffee down on her tray. "I'll help you." He picked up the remote for the bed and lifted the back until she signaled for him to stop. He handed her a cup of coffee and a smile. "They said you can go as soon as you feel strong enough."

She took a sip of her coffee, tasting sugar and a hint of cream. "You know how I take my coffee?"

He ducked his head. "Is it right?"

"It's perfect." She took another sip and though her head ached, and her ribs throbbed, and her leg seemed splintered, she felt better than she had in months.

He settled into the chair next to the bed and drank his own coffee.

"What were you doing at my house?" she asked, not sure why the question had plagued her so fully.

Garth kept his gaze on the floor. "I wanted to make sure you got home okay."

She reached over the bed's railing and put her hand on his arm. "Thank you. You saved me."

He shook his head. "Didn't do anything extraordinary."

She disagreed but didn't argue the point. She knew in the very depths of her soul that if Garth hadn't shown up, she'd be lying in the morgue. Pure panic raced through her for a moment before she caged it the way she'd learned to do all those years ago. She drew a deep breath, held it until she felt in control, and pushed the air out. "I can't go back to that house."

"I know," he said. "I asked some of my cowboys to get over there and clean it up, get it put back together. I called your landlady and said you'd be moving at the end of the month."

She blinked at him.

"I called Chelsea and she said she'd take Grant and Teddy. That way they'll be out on the ranch, and I can take care of them until you're ready to have them back."

She sipped her coffee and put the cup down on the tray. She couldn't look at him, didn't want him to see her heart break. "I have to leave Three Rivers."

"I know," he said again. "I'm having my boys take your stuff to the cabin next to mine."

He didn't get it, and she couldn't make him understand the level of fear she lived with, the constant panic that lurked just beneath her skin. She swung her head toward him but only saw the top of his cowboy hat. "Garth, I can't stay here, not even at the ranch."

"Why not?"

"Because Brad is still alive, and unless he's not, I'm not safe here. *You're* not safe here."

"Let's give it some time, okay?" He finally lifted his chin and met her gaze. "Just come stay out on the ranch until your leg heals. You can't run like that anyway."

She pursed her lips, seeing the logic in his plan, but not liking it. Her stomach squirmed as she nodded. "I guess I'm ready to go, then." She pushed the blanket off her lap and moved her legs slowly toward the edge of the bed.

"Just a second." Garth stood and stepped just outside the room. He returned with a wheelchair and helped her into it. He handed over her coffee cup and strapped her backpack on the chair's handles.

He stopped at the nurse's station, where Juliette signed herself out of the hospital with nothing more than a prescription for the pain. Everything would heal. She knew, because today wasn't the first time she'd endured the radiating pain of a broken rib.

Garth helped her into the truck, filled her prescription, asked her what she wanted to eat for breakfast. She let him take care of her, because she didn't have the mental and physical energy to do it herself. And it felt so good to have someone care enough about her to attend to her needs after a beating. She'd never had that in Montana.

Warmth spread through her, melting the numbness, the iciness. "Thank you, Garth."

"Anytime, Juliette."

She reached for his hand and stole his strength, sighing as he headed out of town and toward the ranch.

Garth kept his eye on Juliette over the next several days, marveling at how fast she got back on her feet. The ankle healed quickly with her dedicated use of the boot the doctor had sent home with her. Her ribs still gave her a lot of trouble, but she plowed on, sifting through the things the cowboys had brought from her house, playing with her dogs, and spending a healthy amount of time sitting on Garth's porch.

Finally, the story he'd been waiting for broke on the news. "Juliette!" he called from the living room, where he'd had the national news on in the background while he put together dinner. He paused the TV and went to help her into the house. "Come see."

"See what?"

He turned the volume up on the TV and pushed play, his heart tripping over its beat. He had friends on the police force in Amarillo, and he'd been waiting for the news of Brad's arrest to be made public so he could prove to Juliette she didn't need to head for the hills.

"Ready?"

She nodded, and he skipped back thirty seconds so she could see the beginning of the story. Once the commercial ended, Brad's picture popped up in the corner of the screen.

"Professional bull rider, Brad Thornton, has been arrested on three counts of domestic abuse, in two states. The trouble started in Texas, where Thornton attacked Juliette Thompson—"

Juliette's tear-stained face filled the screen, and she gasped and stumbled back. Garth braced her against his chest, not quite the reaction he'd been hoping for. "Watch."

"—broken ribs and a near-broken leg," the news anchor continued. "Since Miss Thompson pressed charges, two other women, both residents of Bozeman, Montana, where Thornton lives when he's not touring on the professional rodeo circuit, have come forward with allegations of physical abuse from Thornton, including citations and medical reports that detail broken legs, a broken wrist, internal bleeding, and multiple lacerations to the abdomen. Thornton was arrested early this morning as he left the hospital in Amarillo, and he's being held for questioning. If convicted, he faces up to twenty years in jail."

As the news anchor moved onto the next story, Garth realized how tightly he held Juliette's arms, though she didn't protest. He forced himself to release her and step back. She turned into him, her eyes searching his.

"He's going to jail?"

"For a very long time, Juliette." He touched his mouth to her forehead. "You don't need to leave Three Rivers."

"I don't need to leave Three Rivers," she repeated, her voice tinged with an edge of doubt Garth would deal with later.

"And I called up to Montana, and he filed for divorce a long time ago."

Garth couldn't catalog the emotions streaming across her face, from fear to disbelief to relief. "I'm not married."

He couldn't help the grin stealing across his face. "So everything's settled." He tucked his hands around her waist. "And I'm glad, because I really didn't want you to leave." He leaned down and kissed her, softly at first, probing for permission. She pressed into him, giving her assent, and he deepened the kiss.

"I love you, Juliette," he whispered, his lips catching against hers as he spoke.

She didn't repeat the sentiment back to him, but he felt her love for him in the light tracing of her fingers through his hair and the gentle pressure of her mouth against his.

"I love you too, Garth," she whispered, and his heart soared toward the heavens with those three words.

SNEAK PEEK! THE SEVENTH SERGEANT CHAPTER ONE

*T*he sky surrounding Carly Watters had never seemed so wide, so blue, so threatening. Of course, she hadn't set foot outside the city in half a decade. Her heart pulsed out an extra beat as she made a right turn and faced yet another two-lane highway without a single soul in sight.

The previous veteran care handler had told her Three Rivers Ranch was another forty minutes north of town. Carly had half-thought she'd been kidding. But now, with her orchid satin heels pressing against the accelerator and the minutes ticking by, she realized Lex hadn't exaggerated at all.

Dismay tore through her when her tires met dirt instead of asphalt, and she knew her shoes wouldn't survive more than a couple of steps in the dust and gravel. She'd bought the heels as a graduation gift for herself when she'd finished her social work Master's degree at

TCU a couple of years ago, and they remained the most expensive piece of her wardrobe.

"This is a good job," she breathed to herself as that wide-open sky continued to suffocate her. "It's a promotion—one where you can afford to buy another pair of three hundred dollar shoes. So what if you have to come out to the sticks every couple of weeks? It's going to be fine."

But as she pulled her cute, compact car into the parking lot next to a newer building, a sinking sensation in her stomach spoke that nothing would be fine. Carly pulled up the zipper on her jacket and reached for the file of the veteran she'd come all the way out to this ranch to see: Reese Sanders.

A Sergeant, Reese had suffered massive core injuries from a bombing a few years ago. Carly had already pored over Lex's notes, and she expected to find a "happy-go-lucky veteran who left his wheelchair behind after endless hours of horseback riding."

After she'd read his file, Carly had admired his tenacity, the way he'd clawed himself back from the edge of physical devastation. She'd had a hint of that kind of heartache in her life too, but it tasted bitter in the back of her throat and she painted over it with a fresh layer of lipstick and a smile almost as bright as the near-spring sun.

One of her mother's adages sprang to her mind. *Comparison is the thief of joy.*

Carly had tried to make the words mean something in her life, but with two Mary Poppins Practically Perfect in

Every Way older sisters, and a twin sister that Carly was technically older than, she'd never quite been able to measure up.

Even her choice of social work—of dedicating her life to helping others—had been overshadowed by her twin's acceptance into a Ph.D program.

She locked her car as she clicked across the blessedly paved parking lot, the familiar *ba-beep!* somehow strengthening her to carry out this meeting in her usual cheerful manner. The wind caught her hair and blew the blonde locks around her face. She scrambled for the door handle, the weather pulling at her skirt, her jacket, her file.

Almost like God had pressed the fast-forward button on her life, the wind ripped the folder from Carly's grip. The folder containing all of Reese's accomplishments. The folder the previous handler had warned her not to misplace or rearrange. The folder that symbolized the beginning of her new career.

The weather snatched at the pages, sent them twirling through the air, and Carly could do nothing but watch. All at once, her life resumed its normal pace—all except her pulse, which thundered at four times its normal speed. She swiped for the pages with her hands, stomped on others with her precious heels, even hipped one into the doorjamb to keep it from getting sucked into the open Texas range, never to be seen again.

As she attempted to gather together what pages she could, the crunching of paper behind her attracted her attention. She turned, hoping for a handsome cowboy with exceptional lassoing skills.

She got the handsome cowboy bit about right, and she straightened, forgetting about the need to keep her hip curved into the building.

"Let me help you." He bent to grab a fistful of papers before they could be tornadoed away. When he straightened, his dark eyes sparkled with a smile, causing Carly's chest to squeeze in a good way.

"That must be your purple car." He nodded his cowboy-hatted head toward the parking lot.

Her defenses rose. "I like purple."

The man drank in her orchid heels. "Obviously."

"It gets good gas mileage."

"I'm sure it does." He took a couple of stunted steps forward, his hand outstretched, and understanding flooded her. "I'm Reese Sanders. What can I help you with?"

Instead of answering, she reached for his hand and catalogued the thrill that squirreled down her spine at the contact. Warmth from his skin bled into hers, and she allowed her lips to curve upward. "I'm looking for you, Sergeant Sanders." With a measure of regret she didn't quite understand, she withdrew her fingers from his. "I'm your new veteran care coordinator, Carly Watters."

"Ah." He glanced down at the papers again before pushing them toward her. "These must be Lex's notes." Reese shuffled backward, and it looked like he might fall. Carly automatically reached out to steady him.

The death glare he gave first to her hand on his forearm and then which he speared straight into her eyes left zero doubt about how he felt. She yanked her hand back, heat rising through her chest to her cheeks.

"S-sorry," she mumbled, her pinpoint heels suddenly too small to hold her weight. She sagged into the building again, not caring that it slouched her figure, despite her mother's warning voice in her head. "Can we go in? You were expecting me, right? Lex told me—"

"I've been expectin' you, yeah." He bent and collected a paper stuck against the glass, handed it to her, and entered the building before holding the door open for her. "We can meet in the conference room." He nodded to the right. "Through there."

Carly took a deep breath as she passed him, not because she wanted to get a better sense of his smoky, spicy scent, but because she needed the extra oxygen to settle her nerves. Hadn't she read in that blasted file that Reese resisted help? That the only reason he'd even signed up for services was because someone else had called first?

Once inside the conference room, Carly shoved the papers back into the folder, intending to sort through them and put them back in order when she could be alone. She didn't need him to witness first-hand her OCD when it came to her client's files. She moved to the head of the table and sat down.

"So," she started. "Tell me about your job here."

Reese closed the door and moved to the chair next to hers. He possessed a fluidity in his injury, something Carly hadn't expected. She admired the dark stubble along his jaw and found herself fantasizing about what it would feel like against her cheek. If his lips would be soft in comparison as they touched hers.

Her hand flew to her mouth as she sucked in a breath. She needed to find her center, stop this ridiculous train of crazy thoughts. Reese was a *client*. A veteran she was supposed to help. Nothing more.

"I'm the receptionist here at Courage Reins." Reese spoke with quiet authority, and another traitorous trickle of delight made her skin prickle.

"I answer phones, make appointments, help with the horses. That kind of stuff."

Carly pulled out a random piece of paper from the folder and flipped it over. She clicked her pen into operational mode and wrote something. What, she didn't even know. She just wanted to look official, like she knew what she was doing. "You live in Three Rivers?"

"Yeah."

"You drive out here everyday?"

"Everyday I want to get paid."

Carly glanced up from her chicken scratch at the gruff amusement in his voice. His dark diamond eyes studied her, unsettling her and making her next question abandon her mind. Heat rumbled through her stomach, rising until it settled in her face. She shoved the useless notes back into the folder. "What can I help you with, Sergeant Sanders?"

He leaned away from the table, his injury nowhere

near his impressive biceps. The biceps that bulged as he crossed his arms and continued watching her with those gorgeous eyes. He seemed to be able to see right through her pretended professionalism.

"I don't need help," he said. "I'm doin' great. That's what I told Lex a month ago, when she said she was leavin'."

"It's procedure when a new care coordinator—"

Reese lifted one hand, rendering her silent. "I know," he said. "I get it. But I don't need anything right now. I'm good."

Oh, he was. Carly licked her lips and pressed them together, a slim vein of frustration sliding through her. She'd driven two hours for him to tell her he was good?

"Well, maybe I can get some groceries for you on my way back through town."

"I do all my shopping online."

Her eyebrows shot up. "You do your grocery shopping online?"

"You say that like I don't know how to use a computer." A deep chuckle accompanied the words. "It's easy, Miss Carly. You just login to this app, order what you want, and show up at the store. They bring everything right to me. I don't even get out of my truck."

Of course he'd drive a truck. Probably one of those huge, obnoxious pick-ups that she could never see around. Still, she wanted to hear him say *Miss Carly* over and over.

She cleared her throat and straightened the already-straight file. "You sure there's nothing you need? I could stick something in the oven, start a sprinkler, get your mail—"

His arms uncrossed and his left hand came down on hers. "Miss Carly, I don't need anything. But if you wanted to hang around here for a while, I could show you the horses."

Panic streamed through her, mixing with a wild thread of joy at his touch. She could hardly sort through how to feel, not to mention what to say.

Finally, her mind came up with *He needs company*. And she could give him that, if nothing else.

"I—Okay," she said. "But I don't think I've ever seen a horse up close."

He looked at her like she'd just said she wasn't human. "Well, Miss Carly, that simply won't do." He pushed against the table and stood. Carly noticed the weakness in his core, the difference in length between his left leg and his right. Even with his injuries, he radiated power and confidence as he reached the door and opened it.

Reese paused on the threshold. "Well? Come on. You can't leave Three Rivers without seeing at least one horse."

Reese had no idea why he'd invited Carly Watters to stay and see the horses. Even more surprising was that she'd agreed. He'd watched her war with something within, but in the end, she'd said yes.

Why'd you ask her at all? he wondered for the fifth time as he stepped onto the dirt road that led to the horse barn. He didn't know. But he did like her bright, blue eyes, her platinum hair, her purple car.

"So tell me about you," he said. "I'm sure that file gives you all my details."

"Six older brothers," Carly said. "From Amarillo. Served two deployments." Her voice caught on the last word, and Reese slid her a glance. She seemed mortified by what she'd said.

"I know I served in the Army," he said. "I know I got hurt. It's okay to talk about."

"Is it?" She peered at him like she wasn't really sure.

"Yeah, sure." Lex had assured him that her replacement was amazing. That she'd take good care of him. Reese didn't need a lot now that he'd gotten the job at Courage Reins, now that he'd signed up for free shipping and online grocery shopping. But he missed Lex. She'd always been good company for him. He wondered if his file said that.

Lonely. A sad, lonely veteran whose best friends have four legs and long manes. Or are already married.

"How long have you been a care coordinator?" he asked, glad when his voice didn't betray the storm of emotions stirring inside.

She gave a nervous giggle. "This is my first appointment." She froze on the gravel, and he thought she'd hurt herself in those bright heels. "I'm totally doing it wrong, aren't I?"

Reese retraced his steps back to her and hooked her elbow in his. "'Course not, Miss Carly. You're keeping me company, and that's exactly what I need right now."

She gazed up at him, and Reese's mind went into a tailspin. His pulse followed suit, and he forced himself to look away so he wouldn't say or do something stupid. He took a slow step toward the barn, relieved when Carly came with him.

He hadn't dated since he'd come home broken, three years ago. Hadn't even thought about it. Had told Chelsea no over and over when she suggested women he could take out. But now, with Carly's cold fingers pressing into his forearm, he thought maybe he was ready to take a step toward getting to know her.

"So, you?" he asked. "I do have six brothers, and they're all married and successful. Does my file say that? That I'm seventh best? The seventh sergeant in the family?"

She shook her head, her loose curls brushing his arm. Fireworks tumbled up his arm and sparked in his shoulder. He hadn't felt like this about anyone for so, so long. He hardly trusted himself to know what it meant.

"No, your file lists your family stats, but nothing about them. Where are they?"

Reese took a deep breath as they stepped out of the weak sunshine and into the barn. Just the presence of animals settled him. "You're not getting out of telling me about yourself." He led her past the first stall, heading for

Elvis. He clucked his tongue at the black-and-white paint stallion.

"Oh, he's gorgeous," Carly breathed as the horse lumbered toward them.

Reese let Elvis snuffle against his hand. "He's a thoroughbred. Won a few races before he hurt his leg." He spoke with love and reverence about the horse. "I rescued him from death. When a racehorse can't race...." He let the sentence hang there, grateful the gentle animal hadn't lost his life.

He'd been saved, the same way Reese had. Though he'd struggled to find worth inside himself, he saw it in Elvis, and he knew God had rescued them both. It had taken Reese many long months to get to that place, and a sense of gratitude filled him every time he thought about his journey.

Elvis eyed Carly, and she shrank behind Reese. "Oh, come on, Miss Carly. He won't bite."

"He's taller than I thought."

Reese turned around. "Let's go see Tabasco. He's smaller."

She went with him, sure and strong on such skinny heels. "Who names the horses?"

"Whoever owns them as foals. We don't get a lot of those here on the ranch. Our horses are retired from working or whatever. We use them for therapy." Further down the line, Tabasco waited with his head already over the fence.

"See? He's much shorter."

Carly reached hesitantly toward him, and Reese willed the bay to behave. He did, his eyes falling halfway closed as Carly stroked his cheek.

"He likes you."

Carly beamed under the compliment, and Reese wanted to make her feel like that again. "So, your family?"

"I have three sisters. Two older, and one twin, who I'm four minutes older than."

"A twin, huh?"

"Mirror twins," she said. "My hair parts on the left, hers on the right. I have a dimple on my left cheek, hers is on the right."

Reese had no idea what mirror twins meant, but before he could ask more, she said, "Basically everything Cassie does is right, while everything I do isn't."

He heard every syllable of resentment, of frustration, of sadness in her statement. In her next breath, she put on a happy smile and started asking him about the different kinds of horses.

Reese obliged and kept the conversation light and flowing. But he couldn't shake the feeling that maybe Carly Watters was as lonely as he was.

Second Chance Ranch: A Three Rivers Ranch Romance (Book 1): After his deployment, injured and discharged Major Squire Ackerman returns to Three Rivers Ranch, wanting to forgive Kelly for ignoring him a decade ago. He'd like to provide the stable life she needs, but with old wounds opening and a ranch on the brink of financial collapse, it will take patience and faith to make their second chance possible.

Third Time's the Charm: A Three Rivers Ranch Romance (Book 2): First Lieutenant Peter Marshall has a truckload of debt and no way to provide for a family, but Chelsea helps him see past all the obstacles, all the scars. With so many unknowns, can Pete and Chelsea develop the love, acceptance, and faith needed to find their happily ever after?

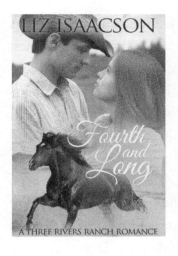

Fourth and Long: A Three Rivers Ranch Romance (Book 3): Commander Brett Murphy goes to Three Rivers Ranch to find some rest and relaxation with his Army buddies. Having his ex-wife show up with a seven-year-old she claims is his son is anything but the R&R he craves. Kate needs to make amends, and Brett needs to find forgiveness, but are they too late to find their happily ever after?

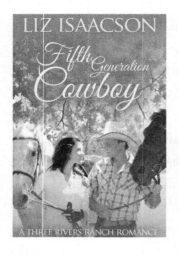

Fifth Generation Cowboy: A Three Rivers Ranch Romance (Book 4): Tom Lovell has watched his friends find their true happiness on Three Rivers Ranch, but everywhere he looks, he only sees friends. Rose Reyes has been bringing her daughter out to the ranch for equine therapy for months, but it doesn't seem to be working. Her challenges with Mari are just as frustrating as ever. Could Tom be exactly what Rose needs? Can he remove his friendship blinders and find love with someone who's been right in front of him all this time?

Sixth Street Love Affair: A Three Rivers Ranch Romance (Book 5): After losing his wife a few years back, Garth Ahlstrom thinks he's ready for a second chance at love. But Juliette Thompson has a secret that could destroy their budding relationship. Can they find the strength, patience, and faith to make things work?

The Seventh Sergeant: A Three Rivers Ranch Romance (Book 6): Life has finally started to settle down for Sergeant Reese Sanders after his devastating injury overseas. Discharged from the Army and now with a good job at Courage Reins, he's finally found happiness—until a horrific fall puts him right back where he was years ago: Injured and depressed. Carly Watters, Reese's new veteran care coordinator, dislikes small towns almost as much as she loathes cowboys. But she finds herself faced with both when she gets assigned to Reese's case. Do they have the humility and faith to make their relationship more than professional?

Eight Second Ride: A Three Rivers Ranch Romance (Book 7): Ethan Greene loves his work at Three Rivers Ranch, but he can't seem to find the right woman to settle down with. When sassy yet vulnerable Brynn Bowman shows up at the ranch to recruit him back to the rodeo circuit, he takes a different approach with the barrel racing champion. His patience and newfound faith pay off when a friendship--and more--starts with Brynn. But she wants out of the rodeo circuit right when Ethan wants to rejoin. Can they find the path God wants them to take and still stay together?

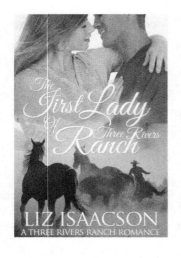

The First Lady of Three Rivers Ranch: A Three Rivers Ranch Romance (Book 8): Heidi Duffin has been dreaming about opening her own bakery since she was thirteen years old. She scrimped and saved for years to afford baking and pastry school in San Francisco. And now she only has one year left before she's a certified pastry chef. Frank Ackerman's father has recently retired, and he's taken over the largest cattle ranch in the Texas Panhandle. A horseman through and through, he's also nearing thirty-one and looking for someone to bring love and joy to a homestead that's been dominated by men for a decade. But when he convinces Heidi to come clean the cowboy cabins, she changes all that. But the siren's call of a bakery is still loud in Heidi's ears, even if she's also seeing a future with Frank. Can she rely on her faith in ways she's never had to before or will their relationship end when summer does?

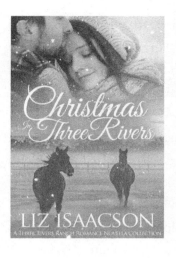

Christmas in Three Rivers: A Three Rivers Ranch Romance (Book 9): Isn't Christmas the best time to fall in love? The cowboys of Three Rivers Ranch think so. Join four of them as they journey toward their path to happily ever after in four, all-new novellas in the Amazon #1 Bestselling Three Rivers Ranch Romance series.

THE NINTH INNING: The Christmas season has never felt like such a burden to boutique owner Andrea Larsen. But with Mama gone and the holidays upon her, Andy finds herself wishing she hadn't been so quick to judge her former boyfriend, cowboy Lawrence Collins. Well, Lawrence hasn't forgotten about Andy either, and he devises a plan to get her out to the ranch so they can reconnect. Do they have the faith and humility to patch things up and start a new relationship?

TEN DAYS IN TOWN: Sandy Keller is tired of the dating scene in Three Rivers. Though she owns the pancake house, she's looking for a fresh start, which means an escape from the town where she grew up. When her older brother's best friend, Tad Jorgensen, comes to town for the holidays, it is a balm to his weary soul. A helicopter tour guide who experienced a near-death experience, he's looking to start over too--but in Three Rivers. Can Sandy and Tad navigate their troubles to find the path God wants them to take--and discover true love--in only ten days?

ELEVEN YEAR REUNION: Pastry chef extraordinaire, Grace Lewis has moved to Three Rivers to help Heidi Ackerman open a bakery in Three Rivers. Grace relishes the idea of starting over in a town where no one knows about her failed cupcakery. She doesn't expect to run into her old high school boyfriend, Jonathan Carver. A carpenter working at Three Rivers Ranch, Jon's in town against his will. But with Grace now on the scene, Jon's thinking life in Three Rivers is suddenly looking up. But with her focus on baking and his disdain for small towns, can they make their eleven year reunion stick?

THE TWELFTH TOWN: Newscaster Taryn Tucker has had enough of life on-screen. She's bounced from town to town before arriving in Three Rivers, completely alone and completely anonymous--just the way she now likes it. She takes a job cleaning at Three Rivers Ranch, hoping for a chance to figure out who she is and where God wants her. When she meets happy-go-lucky cowhand Kenny Stockton, she doesn't expect sparks to fly. Kenny's always been "the best friend" for his female friends, but the pull between him and Taryn can't be denied. Will they have the courage and faith necessary to make their opposite worlds mesh?

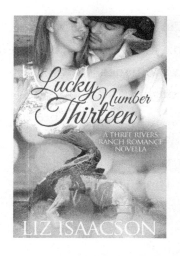

Lucky Number Thirteen: A Three Rivers Ranch Romance (Book 10): Tanner Wolf, a rodeo champion ten times over, is excited to be riding in Three Rivers for the first time since he left his philandering ways and found religion. Seeing his old friends Ethan and Brynn is therapuetic--until a terrible accident lands him in the hospital. With his rodeo career over, Tanner thinks maybe he'll stay in town--and it's not just because his nurse, Summer Hamblin, is the prettiest woman he's ever met. But Summer's the queen of first dates, and as she looks for a way to make a relationship with the transient rodeo star work Summer's not sure she has the fortitude to go on a second date. Can they find love among the tragedy?

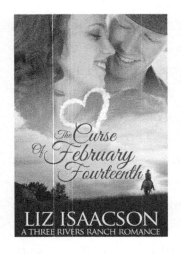

The Curse of February Fourteenth: A Three Rivers Ranch Romance (Book 11): Cal Hodgkins, cowboy veterinarian at Bowman's Breeds, isn't planning to meet anyone at the masked dance in small-town Three Rivers. He just wants to get his bachelor friends off his back and sit on the sidelines to drink his punch. But when he sees a woman dressed in gorgeous butterfly wings and cowgirl boots with blue stitching, he's smitten. Too bad she runs away from the dance before he can get her name, leaving only her boot behind...

Fifteen Minutes of Fame: A Three Rivers Ranch Romance (Book 12): Navy Richards is thirty-five years of tired—tired of dating the same men, working a demanding job, and getting her heart broken over and over again. Her aunt has always spoken highly of the matchmaker in Three Rivers, Texas, so she takes a six-month sabbatical from her high-stress job as a pediatric nurse, hops on a bus, and meets with the matchmaker. Then she meets Gavin Redd. He's handsome, he's hardworking, and he's a cowboy. But is he an Aquarius too? Navy's not making a move until she knows for sure...

Sixteen Steps to Fall in Love: A Three Rivers Ranch Romance (Book 13): A chance encounter at a dog park sheds new light on the tall, talented Boone that Nicole can't ignore. As they get to know each other better and start to dig into each other's past, Nicole is the one who wants to run. This time from her growing admiration and attachment to Boone. From her aging parents. From herself.

But Boone feels the attraction between them too, and he decides he's tired of running and ready to make Three Rivers his permanent home. **Can Boone and Nicole use their faith to overcome their differences and find a happily-ever-after together?**

The Sleigh on Seventeenth Street: A Three Rivers Ranch Romance (Book 14): A cowboy with skills as an electrician tries a relationship with a down-on-her luck plumber. Can Dylan and Camila make water and electricity play nicely together this Christmas season? Or will they get shocked as they try to make their relationship work?

BOOKS IN THE CHRISTMAS IN CORAL CANYON ROMANCE SERIES

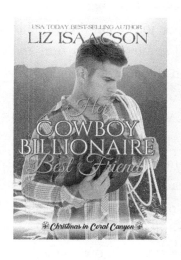

Her Cowboy Billionaire Best Friend (Book 1): Graham Whittaker returns to Coral Canyon a few days after Christmas—after the death of his father. He takes over the energy company his dad built from the ground up and buys a high-end lodge to live in—only a mile from the home of his once-best friend, Laney McAllister. They were best friends once, but Laney's always entertained feelings for him, and spending so much time with him while they make Christmas memories puts her heart in danger of getting broken again…

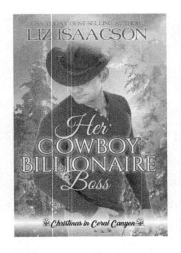

Her Cowboy Billionaire Boss (Book 2): Since the death of his wife a few years ago, Eli Whittaker has been running from one job to another, unable to find somewhere for him and his son to settle. Meg Palmer is Stockton's nanny, and she comes with her boss, Eli, to the lodge, her long-time crush on the man no different in Wyoming than it was on the beach. When she confesses her feelings for him and gets nothing in return, she's crushed, embarrassed, and unsure if she can stay in Coral Canyon for Christmas. Then Eli starts to show some feelings for her too...

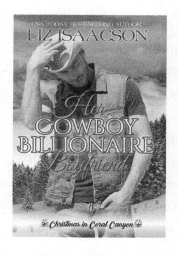

Her Cowboy Billionaire Boyfriend (Book 3): Andrew Whittaker is the public face for the Whittaker Brothers' family energy company, and with his older brother's robot about to be announced, he needs a press secretary to help him get everything ready and tour the state to make the announcements. When he's hit by a protest sign being carried by the company's biggest opponent, Rebecca Collings, he learns with a few clicks that she has the background they need. He offers her the job of press secretary when she thought she was going to be arrested, and not only because the spark between them in so hot Andrew can't see straight.

Can Becca and Andrew work together and keep their relationship a secret? Or will hearts break in this classic romance retelling reminiscent of *Two Weeks Notice*?

Her Cowboy Billionaire Bodyguard (Book 4): Beau Whittaker has watched his brothers find love one by one, but every attempt he's made has ended in disaster. Lily Everett has been in the spotlight since childhood and has half a dozen platinum records with her two sisters. She's taking a break from the brutal music industry and hiding out in Wyoming while her ex-husband continues to cause trouble for her. When she hears of Beau Whittaker and what he offers his clients, she wants to meet him. Beau is instantly attracted to Lily, but he tried a relationship with his last client that left a scar that still hasn't healed…

Can Lily use the spirit of Christmas to discover what matters most? Will Beau open his heart to the possibility of love with someone so different from him?

Her Cowboy Billionaire Bull Rider (Book 5): Todd Christopherson has just retired from the professional rodeo circuit and returned to his hometown of Coral Canyon. Problem is, he's got no family there anymore, no land, and no job. Not that he needs a job--he's got plenty of money from his illustrious career riding bulls.

Then Todd gets thrown during a routine horseback ride up the canyon, and his only support as he recovers physically is the beautiful Violet Everett. She's no nurse, but she does the best she can for the handsome cowboy. **Will she lose her heart to the billionaire bull rider? Can Todd trust that God led him to Coral Canyon...and Vi?**

Her Cowboy Billionaire Bachelor (Book 6): Rose Everett isn't sure what to do with her life now that her country music career is on hold. After all, with both of her sisters in Coral Canyon, and one about to have a baby, they're not making albums anymore.

Liam Murphy has been working for Doctors Without Borders, but he's back in the US now, and looking to start a new clinic in Coral Canyon, where he spent his summers.

When Rose wins a date with Liam in a bachelor auction, their relationship blooms and grows quickly. **Can Liam and Rose find a solution to their problems that doesn't involve one of them leaving Coral Canyon with a broken heart?**

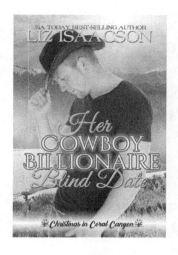

Her Cowboy Billionaire Blind Date (Book 7): Her sons want her to be happy, but she's too old to be set up on a blind date...isn't she?

Amanda Whittaker has been looking for a second chance at love since the death of her husband several years ago. Finley Barber is a cowboy in every sense of the word. Born and raised on a racehorse farm in Kentucky, he's since moved to Dog Valley and started his own breeding stable for champion horses. He hasn't dated in years, and everything about Amanda makes him nervous.

Will Amanda take the leap of faith required to be with Finn? Or will he become just another boyfriend who doesn't make the cut?

Her Cowboy Billionaire Best Man (Book 8): When Celia Abbott-Armstrong runs into a gorgeous cowboy at her best friend's wedding, she decides she's ready to start dating again.

But the cowboy is Zach Zuckerman, and the Zuckermans and Abbotts have been at war for generations.

Can Zach and Celia find a way to reconcile their family's differences so they can have a future together?

Her Cowboy Billionaire Birthday Wish (Book 9): All the maid at Whiskey Mountain Lodge wants for her birthday is a handsome cowboy billionaire. And Colton can make that wish come true—if only he hadn't escaped to Coral Canyon after being left at the altar...

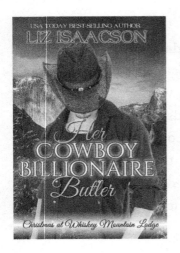

Her Cowboy Billionaire Butler (Book 10): She broke up with him to date another man...who broke her heart. He's a former CEO with nothing to do who can't get her out of his head. Can Wes and Bree find a way toward happily-ever-after at Whiskey Mountain Lodge?

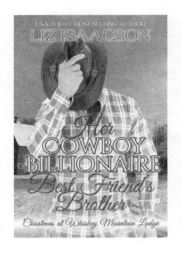

Her Cowboy Billionaire Best Friend's Brother (Book 11): She's best friends with the single dad cowboy's brother and has watched two friends find love with the sexy new cowboys in town. When Gray Hammond comes to Whiskey Mountain Lodge with his son, will Elise finally get her own happily-ever-after with one of the Hammond brothers?

Her Cowboy Billionaire Beast (Book 12): A cowboy billionaire beast, his new manager, and the Christmas traditions that soften his heart and bring them together.

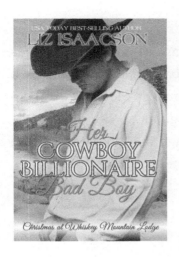

Her Cowboy Billionaire Bad Boy (Book 13): A cowboy billionaire cop who's a stickler for rules, the woman he pulls over when he's not even on duty, and the personal mandates he has to break to keep her in his life...

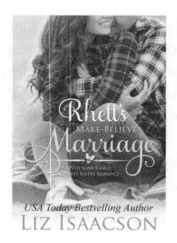

Rhett's Make-Believe Marriage (Book 1): She needs a husband to be credible as a matchmaker. He wants to help a neighbor. Will their fake marriage take them out of the friend zone?

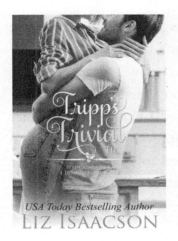

Tripp's Trivial Tie (Book 2): She needs a husband to keep her son. He's wanted to take their relationship to the next level, but she's always pushing him away. Will their trivial tie take them all the way to happily-ever-after?

Liam's Invented I-Do (Book 3): She's desperate to save her ranch. He wants to help her any way he can. Will their invented I-Do open doors that have previously been closed and lead to a happily-ever-after for both of them?

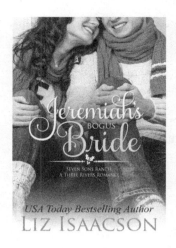

Jeremiah's Bogus Bride (Book 4): He wants to prove to his brothers that he's not broken. She just wants him. Will a fake marriage heal him or push her further away?

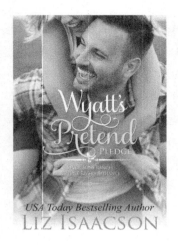

Wyatt's Pretend Pledge (Book 5): To get her inheritance, she needs a husband. He's wanted to fly with her for ages. Can their pretend pledge turn into something real?

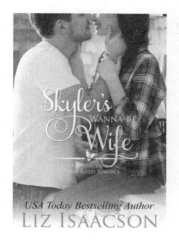

Skyler's Wanna-Be Wife (Book 6): She needs a new last name to stay in school. He's willing to help a fellow student. Can this wanna-be wife show the playboy that some things should be taken seriously?

Micah's Mock Matrimony (Book 7): They were just actors auditioning for a play. The marriage was just for the audition – until a clerical error results in a legal marriage. Can these two ex-lovers negotiate this new ground between them and achieve new roles in each other's lives?

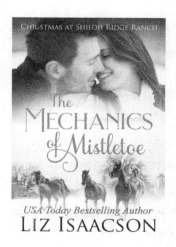

The Mechanics of Mistletoe (Book 1): Bear Glover can be a grizzly or a teddy, and he's always thought he'd be just fine working his generational family ranch and going back to the ancient homestead alone. But his crush on Samantha Benton won't go away. She's a genius with a wrench on Bear's tractors...and his heart. Can he tame his wild side and get the girl, or will he be left broken-hearted this Christmas season?

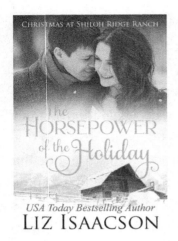

The Horsepower of the Holiday (Book 2): Ranger Glover has worked at Shiloh Ridge Ranch his entire life. The cowboys do everything from horseback there, but when he goes to town to trade in some trucks, somehow Oakley Hatch persuades him to take some ATVs back to the ranch. (Bear is NOT happy.)

She's a former race car driver who's got Ranger all revved up... Can he remember who he is and get Oakley to slow down enough to fall in love, or will there simply be too much horsepower in the holiday this year for a real relationship?

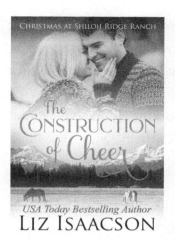

The Construction of Cheer (Book 3): Bishop Glover is the youngest brother, and he usually keeps his head down and gets the job done. When Montana Martin shows up at Shiloh Ridge Ranch looking for work, he finds himself inventing construction projects that need doing just to keep her coming around. (Again, Bear is NOT happy.) She wants to build her own construction firm, but she ends up carving a place for herself inside Bishop's heart. Can he convince her *he's* all she needs this Christmas season, or will her cheer rest solely on the success of her business?

The Secret of Santa (Book 4): Ace Glover loves to laugh, and everywhere he goes, luck seems to follow. When the hardworking cowboy volunteers to help with the Poinsettia Festival in town, he meets Sierra Broadbent. He's instantly smitten and loves spending time with her. She's in charge of the whole event, but she seems to disappear the moment everything starts...day after day.

When he learns her secret, the entire festival could be ruined—and so could Sierra's reputation and his new relationship with her. Will he keep his discovery to himself or will Sierra's secret become front-page news on Christmas Day?

BOOKS IN THE LAST CHANCE RANCH ROMANCE SERIES

Last Chance Ranch (Book 1): A cowgirl down on her luck hires a man who's good with horses and under the hood of a car. Can Hudson fine tune Scarlett's heart as they work together? Or will things backfire and make everything worse at Last Chance Ranch?

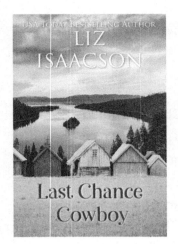

Last Chance Cowboy (Book 2): A billionaire cowboy without a home meets a woman who secretly makes food videos to pay her debts...Can Carson and Adele do more than fight in the kitchens at Last Chance Ranch?

Last Chance Wedding (Book 3): A female carpenter needs a husband just for a few days... Can Jeri and Sawyer navigate the minefield of a pretend marriage before their feelings become real?

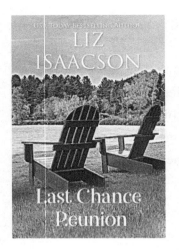

Last Chance Reunion (Book 4): An Army cowboy, the woman he dated years ago, and their last chance at Last Chance Ranch... Can Dave and Sissy put aside hurt feelings and make their second chance romance work?

Last Chance Lake (Book 5): A former dairy farmer and the marketing director on the ranch have to work together to make the cow cuddling program a success. But can Karla let Cache into her life? Or will she keep all her secrets from him - and keep *him* a secret too?

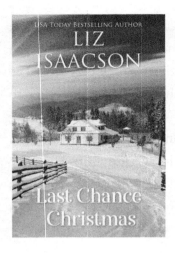

Last Chance Christmas (Book 6): She's tired of having her heart broken by cowboys. He waited too long to ask her out. Can Lance fix things quickly, or will Amber leave Last Chance Ranch before he can tell her how he feels?

BOOKS IN THE GRAPE SEED FALLS ROMANCE SERIES:

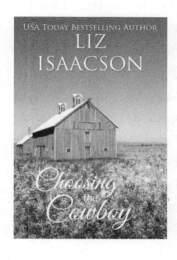

Choosing the Cowboy (Book 1): With financial trouble and personal issues around every corner, can Maggie Duffin and Chase Carver rely on their faith to find their happily-ever-after?

A spinoff from the #1 best-selling Three Rivers Ranch Romance novels, also by USA Today bestselling author Liz Isaacson.

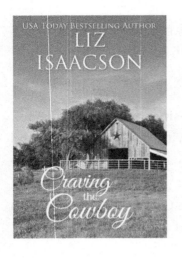

Craving the Cowboy (Book 2): Dwayne Carver is set to inherit his family's ranch in the heart of Texas Hill Country, and in order to keep up with his ranch duties and fulfill his dreams of owning a horse farm, he hires top trainer Felicity Lightburne. They get along great, and she can envision herself on this new farm—at least until her mother falls ill and she has to return to help her. Can Dwayne and Felicity work through their differences to find their happily-ever-after?

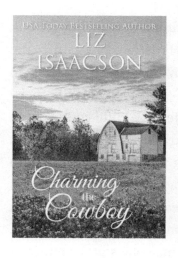

Charming the Cowboy (Book 3): Third grade teacher Heather Carver has had her eye on Levi Rhodes for a couple of years now, but he seems to be blind to her attempts to charm him. When she breaks her arm while on his horse ranch, Heather infiltrates Levi's life in ways he's never thought of, and his strict anti-female stance slips. Will Heather heal his emotional scars and he care for her physical ones so they can have a real relationship?

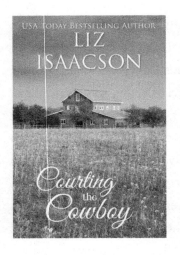

Courting the Cowboy (Book 4): Frustrated with the cowboy-only dating scene in Grape Seed Falls, May Sotheby joins TexasFaithful.com, hoping to find her soul mate without having to relocate--or deal with cowboy hats and boots. She has no idea that Kurt Pemberton, foreman at Grape Seed Ranch, is the man she starts communicating with... Will May be able to follow her heart and get Kurt to forgive her so they can be together?

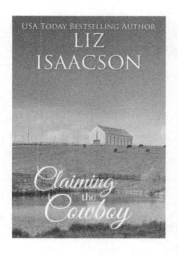

Claiming the Cowboy, Royal Brothers Book 1 (Grape Seed Falls Romance Book 5): Unwilling to be tied down, farrier Robin Cook has managed to pack her entire life into a two-hundred-and-eighty square-foot house, and that includes her Yorkie. Cowboy and co-foreman, Shane Royal has had his heart set on Robin for three years, even though she flat-out turned him down the last time he asked her to dinner. But she's back at Grape Seed Ranch for five weeks as she works her horse-shoeing magic, and he's still interested, despite a bitter life lesson that left a bad taste for marriage in his mouth.

Robin's interested in him too. But can she find room for Shane in her tiny house--and can he take a chance on her with his tired heart?

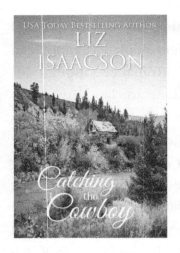**Catching the Cowboy, Royal Brothers Book 2 (Grape Seed Falls Romance Book 6):** Dylan Royal is good at two things: whistling and caring for cattle. When his cows are being attacked by an unknown wild animal, he calls Texas Parks & Wildlife for help. He wasn't expecting a beautiful mammologist to show up, all flirty and fun and everything Dylan didn't know he wanted in his life.

Hazel Brewster has gone on more first dates than anyone in Grape Seed Falls, and she thinks maybe Dylan deserves a second... Can they find their way through wild animals, huge life changes, and their emotional pasts to find their forever future?

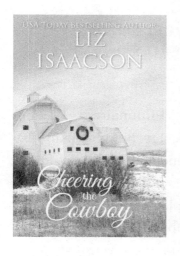

Cheering the Cowboy, Royal Brothers Book 3 (Grape Seed Falls Romance Book 7): Austin Royal loves his life on his new ranch with his brothers. But he doesn't love that Shayleigh Hatch came with the property, nor that he has to take the blame for the fact that he now owns her childhood ranch. They rarely have a conversation that doesn't leave him furious and frustrated--and yet he's still attracted to Shay in a strange, new way.

Shay inexplicably likes him too, which utterly confuses and angers her. As they work to make this Christmas the best the Triple Towers Ranch has ever seen, can they also navigate through their rocky relationship to smoother waters?

BOOKS IN THE STEEPLE RIDGE
ROMANCE SERIES:

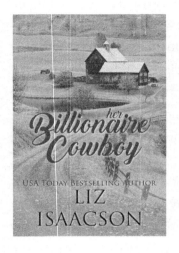

Her Billionaire Cowboy (Book 1): Tucker Jenkins has had enough of tall buildings, traffic, and has traded in his technology firm in New York City for Steeple Ridge Horse Farm in rural Vermont. Missy Marino has worked at the farm since she was a teen, and she's always dreamed of owning it. But her ex-husband left her with a truckload of debt, making her fantasies of owning the farm unfulfilled. Tucker didn't come to the country to find a new wife, but he supposes a woman could help him start over in Steeple Ridge. Will Tucker and Missy be able to navigate the shaky ground between them to find a new beginning?

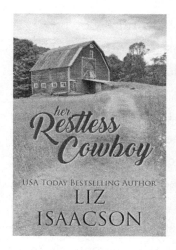

Her Restless Cowboy: A Butters Brothers Novel, Steeple Ridge Romance (Book 2): Ben Buttars is the youngest of the four Buttars brothers who come to Steeple Ridge Farm, and he finally feels like he's landed somewhere he can make a life for himself. Reagan Cantwell is a decade older than Ben and the recreational direction for the town of Island Park. Though Ben is young, he knows what he wants—and that's Rae. Can she figure out how to put what matters most in her life—family and faith—above her job before she loses Ben?

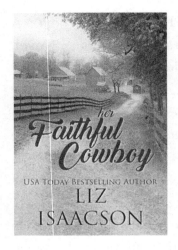

Her Faithful Cowboy: A Butters Brothers Novel, Steeple Ridge Romance (Book 3): Sam Buttars has spent the last decade making sure he and his brothers stay together. They've been at Steeple Ridge for a while now, but with the youngest married and happy, the siren's call to return to his parents' farm in Wyoming is loud in Sam's ears. He'd just go if it weren't for beautiful Bonnie Sherman, who roped his heart the first time he saw her. Do Sam and Bonnie have the faith to find comfort in each other instead of in the people who've already passed?

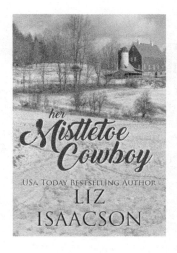

Her Mistletoe Cowboy: A Butters Brothers Novel, Steeple Ridge Romance (Book 4): Logan Buttars has always been good-natured and happy-go-lucky. After watching two of his brothers settle down, he recognizes a void in his life he didn't know about. Veterinarian Layla Guyman has appreciated Logan's friendship and easy way with animals when he comes into the clinic to get the service dogs. But with his future at Steeple Ridge in the balance, she's not sure a relationship with him is worth the risk. Can she rely on her faith and employ patience to tame Logan's wild heart?

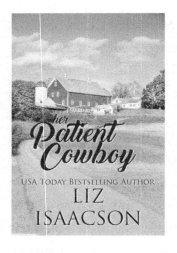

Her Patient Cowboy: A Butters Brothers Novel, Steeple Ridge Romance (Book 5): Darren Buttars is cool, collected, and quiet—and utterly devastated when his girlfriend of nine months, Farrah Irvine, breaks up with him because he wanted her to ride her horse in a parade. But Farrah doesn't ride anymore, a fact she made very clear to Darren. She returned to her childhood home with so much baggage, she doesn't know where to start with the unpacking. Darren's the only Buttars brother who isn't married, and he wants to make Island Park his permanent home—with Farrah. Can they find their way through the heartache to achieve a happily-ever-after together?

BOOKS IN THE HORSESHOE HOME
RANCH ROMANCE SERIES:

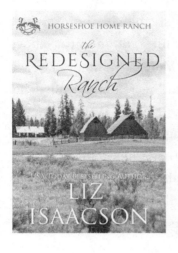

The Redesigned Ranch (Book 1): Jace Lovell only has one thing left after his fiancé abandons him at the altar: his job at Horseshoe Home Ranch. Belle Edmunds is back in Gold Valley and she's desperate to build a portfolio that she can use to start her own firm in Montana. Jace isn't anywhere near forgiving his fiancé, and he's not sure he's ready for a new relationship with someone as fiery and beautiful as Belle. Can she employ her patience while he figures out how to forgive so they can find their own brand of happily-ever-after?

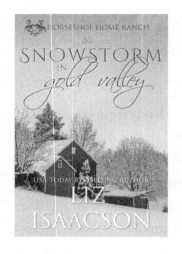

The Snowstorm in Gold Valley (Book 2): Professional snowboarder Sterling Maughan has sequestered himself in his family's cabin in the exclusive mountain community above Gold Valley, Montana after a devastating fall that ended his career. Norah Watson cleans Sterling's cabin and the more time they spend together, the more Sterling is interested in all things Norah. As his body heals, so does his faith. Will Norah be able to trust Sterling so they can have a chance at true love?

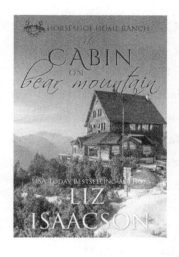

The Cabin on Bear Mountain (Book 3): Landon Edmunds has been a cowboy his whole life. An accident five years ago ended his successful rodeo career, and now he's looking to start a horse ranch--and he's looking outside of Montana. Which would be great if God hadn't brought Megan Palmer back to Gold Valley right when Landon is looking to leave. Megan and Landon work together well, and as sparks fly, she's sure God brought her back to Gold Valley so she could find her happily ever after. Through serious discussion and prayer, can Landon and Megan find their future together?

Be sure to check out the spinoff series, the Brush Creek Brides romances after you read FALLING FOR HIS BEST FRIEND. Start with A WEDDING FOR THE WIDOWER.

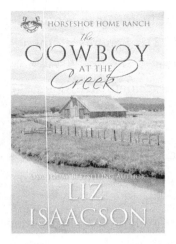

The Cowboy at the Creek (Book 4): Twelve years ago, Owen Carr left Gold Valley—and his long-time girlfriend—in favor of a country music career in Nashville. Married and divorced, Natalie teaches ballet at the dance studio in Gold Valley, but she never auditioned for the professional company the way she dreamed of doing. With Owen back, she realizes all the opportunities she missed out on when he left all those years ago—including a future with him. Can they mend broken bridges in order to have a second chance at love?

The Wedding in the Winter (Book 5): Caleb Chamberlain has spent the last five years recovering from a horrible breakup, his alcoholism that stemmed from it, and the car accident that left him hospitalized. He's finally on the right track in his life—until Holly Gray, his twin brother's ex-fiance mistakes him for Nathan. Holly's back in Gold Valley to get the required veterinarian hours to apply for her graduate program. When the herd at Horseshoe Home comes down with pneumonia, Caleb and Holly are forced to work together in close quarters. Holly's over Nathan, but she hasn't forgiven him—or the woman she believes broke up their relationship. Can Caleb and Holly navigate such a rough past to find their happily-ever-after?

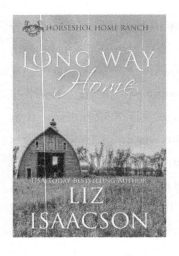

The Long Way Home (Book 6): Ty Barker has been dancing through the last thirty years of his life--and he's suddenly realized he's alone. River Lee Whitely is back in Gold Valley with her two little girls after a divorce that's left deep scars. She has a job at Silver Creek that requires her to be able to ride a horse, and she nearly tramples Ty at her first lesson. That's just fine by him, because River Lee is the girl Ty has never gotten over. Ty realizes River Lee needs time to settle into her new job, her new home, her new life as a single parent, but going slow has never been his style. But for River Lee, can Ty take the necessary steps to keep her in his life?

Christmas at the Ranch (Book 7): Archer Bailey has already lost one job to Emersyn Enders, so he deliberately doesn't tell her about the cowhand job up at Horseshoe Home Ranch. Emery's temporary job is ending, but her obligations to her physically disabled sister aren't. As Archer and Emery work together, its clear that the sparks flying between them aren't all from their friendly competition over a job. Will Emery and Archer be able to navigate the ranch, their close quarters, and their individual circumstances to find love this holiday season?

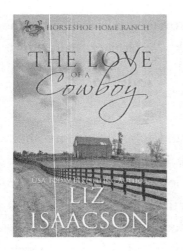

The Love of a Cowboy (Book 8): Cowboy Elliott Hawthorne has just lost his best friend and cabin mate to the worst thing imaginable—marriage. When his brother calls about an accident with their father, Elliott rushes down to Gold Valley from the ranch only to be met with the most beautiful woman he's ever seen. His father's new physical therapist, London Marsh, likes the handsome face and gentle spirit she sees in Elliott too. Can Elliott and London navigate difficult family situations to find a happily-ever-after?

BOOKS IN THE BRUSH CREEK BRIDES ROMANCE SERIES:

Brush Creek Cowboy: Brush Creek Cowboys Romance (Book 1): Former rodeo champion and cowboy Walker Thompson trains horses at Brush Creek Horse Ranch, where he lives a simple life in his cabin with his ten-year-old son. A widower of six years, he's worked with Tess Wagner, a widow who came to Brush Creek to escape the turmoil of her life to give her seven-year-old son a slower pace of life. But Tess's breast cancer is back...

Walker will have to decide if he'd rather spend even a short time with Tess than not have her in his life at all. Tess wants to feel God's love and power, but can she discover and accept God's will in order to find her happy ending?

The Cowboy's Challenge: Brush Creek Brides Romance (Book 2): Cowboy and professional roper Justin Jackman has found solitude at Brush Creek Horse Ranch, preferring his time with the animals he trains over dating. With two failed engagements in his past, he's not really interested in getting his heart stomped on again. But when flirty and fun Renee  Martin picks him up at a church ice cream bar--on a bet, no less--he finds himself more than just a little interested. His Gen-X attitudes are attractive to her; her Millennial behaviors drive him nuts. Can Justin look past their differences and take a chance on another engagement?

A Cowboy Proposal: Brush Creek Brides Romance (Book 3): Ted Caldwell has been a retired bronc rider for years, and he thought he was perfectly happy training horses to buck at Brush Creek Ranch. He was wrong. When he meets April Nox, who comes to the ranch to hide her pregnancy from all her friends back in Jackson Hole, Ted realizes he has a huge family-shaped hole in his life. April is embarrassed, heartbroken, and trying to find her extinguished faith. She's never ridden a horse and wants nothing to do with a cowboy ever again. Can Ted and April create a family of happiness and love from a tragedy?

A New Family for the Cowboy: Brush Creek Brides Romance (Book 4): Blake Gibbons oversees all the agriculture at Brush Creek Horse Ranch, sometimes moonlighting as a general contractor. When he meets Erin Shields, new in town, at her aunt's bakery, he's instantly smitten. Erin moved to Brush Creek after a divorce that left her  penniless, homeless, and a single mother of three children under age eight. She's nowhere near ready to start dating again, but the longer Blake hangs around the bakery, the more she starts to like him. Can Blake and Erin find a way to blend their lifestyles and become a family?

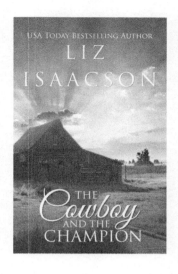

The Cowboy and the Champion: Brush Creek Brides Romance (Book 5): Emmett Graves has always had a positive outlook on life. He adores training horses to become barrel racing champions during the day and cuddling with his cat at night. Fresh off her professional rodeo retirement, Molly Brady comes to Brush Creek Horse Ranch as Emmett's protege. He's not thrilled, and she's allergic to cats. Oh, and she'd like to stay cowboy-free, thank you very much. But Emmett's about as cowboy as they come…. Can Emmett and Molly work together without falling in love?

Schooled by the Cowboy: Brush Creek Brides Romance (Book 6): Grant Ford spends his days training cattle—when he's not camped out at the elementary school hoping to catch a glimpse of his ex-girlfriend. When principal Shannon Sharpe confronts him and asks him to stay away from the school, the spark between them is instant and hot. Shannon's expecting a transfer very soon, but she also needs a summer outdoor coordinator—and Grant fits the bill. Just because he's handsome and everything Shannon's ever wanted in a cowboy husband means nothing. Will Grant and Shannon be able to survive the summer or will the Utah heat be too much for them to handle?

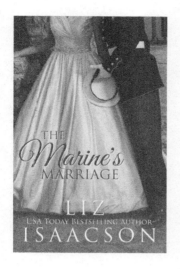

The Marine's Marriage: A Fuller Family Novel - Brush Creek Brides Romance (Book 1): Tate Benson can't believe he's come to Nowhere, Utah, to fix up a house that hasn't been inhabited in years. But he has. Because he's retired from the Marines and looking to start a life as a police officer in small-town Brush Creek. Wren Fuller has her hands full most days running her family's company. When Tate calls and demands a maid for that morning, she decides to have the calls forwarded to her cell and go help him out. She didn't know he was moving in next door, and she's completely unprepared for his handsomeness, his kind heart, and his wounded soul.Can Tate and Wren weather a relationship when they're also next-door neighbors?

The Firefighter's Fiancé: A Fuller Family Novel - Brush Creek Brides Romance (Book 2): Cora Wesley comes to Brush Creek, hoping to get some in-the-wild firefighting training as she prepares to put in her application to be a hotshot. When she meets Brennan Fuller, the spark between them is hot and instant. As they get to know 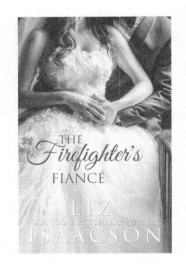 each other, her deadline is constantly looming over them, and Brennan starts to wonder if he can break ranks in the family business. He's okay mowing lawns and hanging out with his brothers, but he dreams of being able to go to college and become a landscape architect, but he's just not sure it can be done. Will Cora and Brennan be able to endure their trials to find true love?

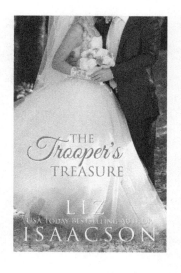

The Trooper's Treasure: A Fuller Family Novel - Brush Creek Brides Romance (Book 3): Dawn Fuller has made some mistakes in her life, and she's not proud of the way McDermott Boyd found her off the road one day last year. She's spent a hard year wrestling with her choices and trying to fix them, glad for McDermott's acceptance and friendship. He lost his wife years ago, done his best with his daughter, and now he's ready to move on. Can McDermott help Dawn find a way past her former mistakes and down a path that leads to love, family, and happiness?

The Detective's Date: A Fuller Family Novel - Brush Creek Brides Romance (Book 4): Dahlia Reid is one of the best detectives Brush Creek and the surrounding towns has ever had. She's given up on the idea of marriage—and pleasing her mother—and has dedicated herself fully to her job. Which is great, since one of the most perplexing cases of her career 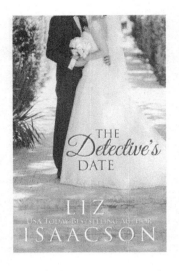 has come to town. Kyler Fuller thinks he's finally ready to move past the woman who ghosted him years ago. He's cut his hair, and he's ready to start dating. Too bad every woman he's been out with is about as interesting as a lamppost—until Dahlia. He finds her beautiful, her quick wit a breath of fresh air, and her intelligence sexy. Can Kyler and Dahlia use their faith to find a way through the obstacles threatening to keep them apart?

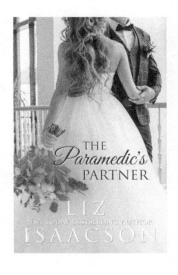

The Paramedic's Partner: A Fuller Family Novel - Brush Creek Brides Romance (Book 5): Jazzy Fuller has always been overshadowed by her prettier, more popular twin, Fabiana. Fabi meets paramedic Max Robinson at the park and sets a date with him only to come down with the flu. So she convinces Jazzy to cut her hair and take her place on the date. And the spark between Jazzy and Max is hot and instant...if only he knew she wasn't her sister, Fabi.

Max drives the ambulance for the town of Brush Creek with is partner Ed Moon, and neither of them have been all that lucky in love. Until Max suggests to who he thinks is Fabi that they should double with Ed and Jazzy. They do, and Fabi is smitten with the steady, strong Ed Moon. As each twin falls further and further in love with their respective paramedic, it becomes obvious they'll need to come clean about the switcheroo sooner rather than later...or risk losing their hearts.

The Chief's Catch: A Fuller Family Novel - Brush Creek Brides Romance (Book 6): Berlin Fuller has struck out with the dating scene in Brush Creek more times than she cares to admit. When she makes a deal with her friends that they can choose the next man she goes out with, she didn't dream they'd pick surly Cole Fairbanks, the new Chief of Police.

His friends call him the Beast and challenge him to complete ten dates that summer or give up his bonus check. When Berlin approaches him, stuttering about the deal with her friends and claiming they don't actually have to go out, he's intrigued. As the summer passes, Cole finds himself burning both ends of the candle to keep up with his job and his new relationship. When he unleashes the Beast one time too many, Berlin will have to decide if she can tame him or if she should walk away.

ABOUT LIZ

Liz Isaacson writes inspirational romance, usually set in Texas, or Montana, or anywhere else horses and cowboys exist. She lives in Utah, where she walks her dogs daily, watches a lot of Netflix, and eats a lot of peanut butter M&Ms while writing. Find her on her website at lizisaacson.com.

Made in the USA
Monee, IL
06 November 2023

45887049R00111